Star Trek: Dark Universe

Written by
Craig Morrin

Copyright © 2022, 2025

While acknowledging Paramount Global's rights to the Star Trek franchise, and all of the names and characters therein, the author of this script claims all of the intellectual property rights related to this unique storyline. The author has not—nor ever intends—to publish this manuscript independently for profit.

A Star Trek "Primer"

In the 2009 movie, *Star Trek,* a temporal incursion occurred that created a whole new universe splitting off of the original Prime Universe in what is now known as the Kelvin Timeline. This story is set entirely in that timeline, with the Kelvin versions of each of those characters from the original universe, each with their own unique destinies and played by a whole new cast of actors, including Chris Pine as the new Captain Kirk.

It is my understanding that the Kelvin Timeline would have also created its own mirror universe. So we actually have four universes: the Prime Universe, the Prime Mirror Universe, the Kelvin Universe, and the Kelvin Mirror Universe. Not only that, but I believe that the temporal incursion that occurred in 2233 would have created Kelvin versions of every Star Trek character, not only in the future...*but also in the past,* including the Kelvin version of the Empress Hoshi Sato of the 22nd century with a completely different destiny from her original counterpart in the Prime Mirror Universe. While the Kelvin versions often share similar characteristics as their Prime counterparts, it can take only one tiny, seemingly insignificant experience to shift them into a vastly different life and destiny...

I realize that all of this might be hard to follow. So instead of spewing more Star Trek technobabble at you, I will attempt to *show* how all of this could be true... through a unique and realistic story that I believe will keep you on the edge of your seat. Fair use allows for the limited use of copyrighted materials if it is for non-profit and educational purposes. And there is no reason why it can't be both educational and entertaining at the same time!

This story begins where *Star Trek Beyond* ends, with the new Captain Kirk (Chris Pine) and the rest of his crew, set in the Kelvin Universe of the 23rd century. But it also intertwines with two other spacetime realities: the 24th century with the Kelvin versions of Jean-Luc Picard and Katheryn Janeway, and the 22nd century with the Kelvin version of the Terran Empire in the mirror universe...all converging to a final showdown that will determine the fate of the entire multiverse. And...not only that, but the original Captain Kirk (William Shatner) from the Prime Universe finds his way into the picture. Sounds too crazy to make for a realistic story? To the best of my knowledge, this script follows true Star Trek canon, not only building off of the latest Star Trek movie, but also *Star Trek: Generations,* "The Tholian Web", "In a Mirror, Darkly", and "Coda." And not only that, but it does not conflict with more recent shows, including *Picard.* This script delves into an area of the Star Trek Universe that has never been touched upon before. We have seen the alternate Kelvin timeline during Captain Kirk's life, but we know nothing about this timeline during Picard and Janeway's lifetimes. Until now.

If you would like to watch the trailers to the aforementioned movies and episodes to get more familiar with the backstory to this script, you can go to www.PrecisionPyramids.com and click on "DARK U" up at the top.

It is pitch black.

Indistinct, fluttering noises can be heard in the darkness.

Gradually, the source of the noises begins to reveal itself: at first, only a single, wispy, ribbon of light, faintly wavering in the darkness. Barely visible, it seems to be coming from out of something...

We see that it is coming from out of the chest of a person, lying comatose upon what looks to be a cold, dark slab of black granite.

The fluttering noises get louder as more bodies are seen, each lying upon their individual black slabs in the darkness, each with a ribbon of light wavering from out of its chest.

At first, only several bodies are seen. Then hundreds. Then millions upon millions of them. Then more than could ever be counted: rows upon rows of comatose bodies that seem to go on into forever towards the distant horizon...each with a wavering ribbon of light coming from out of its chest.

The ribbons of light all seem to be going up, moving and rippling high above the bodies towards some indistinct ocean of energy bathed in an orange-white glow.

We start to move away from all of the comatose bodies, moving up through all of the ribbons of energy fluttering in the air all around us. As we get closer to the rippling ocean of energy above us, it seems to become more turbulent and chaotic...

In a flash, as we move through it, we catch a quick glimpse of what seem to be thousands upon thousands of swarming beings, made up of bright white light in an orange ocean of energy, all feeding upon the ribbons of energy coming from the comatose people below them...but we move so fast through this layer, that it is hard to be certain what it was that we saw.

We come out to the other side, continuing to move farther away, and we see that it is the Nexus, bigger than ever before, as it approaches Earth...

It dwarfs the darkened planet, and as it gets closer, we see a fleet of super-advanced ships in front of it. These are not Starfleet ships. They have the insignia of the Terran Empire upon them—a sword cutting through the earth—revealing that we are in the mirror universe.

The Nexus continues to approach Earth, seemingly oblivious of the ships as it consumes them all in hundreds of fiery explosions...

Jean-Luc Picard is strapped down to some sort of torture apparatus. The insignia of the Terran Empire is upon his uniform. His face has many creases and scars upon it from a life of struggle and strain.

A Terran inquisitor questions him: "Tell us what you know about the Federation Alliance!" PICARD: "The Federation no longer exists! I am a captain of the Terran Empire!" INQUISITOR: "You lie! You are a secret rebel of the Federation Alliance, trying to destroy the Empire!"

The inquisitor pushes a button, and electric jolts pulse through Picard's body as he silently writhes in pain. Then, everything lights up and is enveloped in the orange-white glow of the Nexus as Picard shouts: "*NOOOOOOOO!!!!*"

In the middle of his shout, Picard wakes up in his bed, in the normal universe, shouting: "*NOOOOOOOO!!!!*"

[Normal universe, 23rd century, Kelvin timeline]
We see the new USS *Enterprise* (NCC-1701-A) being built in fast motion as we hear the voice of a young Captain Kirk: "Captain's log: Stardate 2264.5. Construction of the new Enterprise-A has finally finished, and I feel that my crew is ready and eager to begin our five-year mission into the Robidian Nebula..."

The scene switches to young Kirk and Spock standing next to each other as the turbolift is moving. They are not talking, and there is a slightly noticeable look of discomfort in Spock's demeanor. SPOCK: "Captain." KIRK: "Spock." There is a moment of silence as the turbolift continues to move. Kirk glances at Spock and notices his demeanor. They both speak at the same time. KIRK: "Is every—" SPOCK: "Captain, I need to talk—" The turbolift doors open up to the Bridge. KIRK: "What is it, Spock?" Spock looks uncertain as he stands there, looking at the crew working on all of the different consoles in front of him. SPOCK: "It's nothing." Kirk looks at him for a moment as Spock waits for him to enter the Bridge. Kirk enters, and Spock follows him.

Various members of the *Enterprise* crew are on the Bridge, working at different consoles, including Sulu, Uhura, and others. As Spock approaches his workstation, Uhura flashes him a nasty glance. SULU: "Captain on the Bridge!" Kirk walks towards the captain's chair, and he sits in it with a satisfied expression upon his face. KIRK: "At ease, Sulu." Kirk continues to feel the chair, as if it were a living thing. After a moment, Kirk picks up the intercom, addressing the crew of the *Enterprise*. KIRK: "This is Captain Kirk, here. It has been a long time coming, but I think it will have been well worth the wait. You are seasoned veterans now, and before we embark into the Robidian Nebula and into the greatest adventure that has ever been assigned to a Starfleet crew, we need to test our new ship and to stretch her legs. This is just going to be a short run to investigate the disappearance of the USS Defiant at its last known coordinates." Kirk turns off the intercom. KIRK: "All right, Sulu. Let's open her up and see what she's got." SULU: "Yes, sir!" Sulu starts to move levers on his console. KIRK: "Oh, and Sulu…" Sulu looks up from what he is doing. SULU: "Yes, sir?" Kirk smiles mischievously at him. KIRK: "Don't forget to take the parking brake off this time." Sulu's face turns a little red and he looks back down, continuing to work the levers. SULU: "Never again, sir." *(pause)* "Waiting for your command…" KIRK: "Punch it."

～～～～

The *Enterprise-A* is in an unknown region of space, at the last known coordinates of the USS *Defiant*. It is uncharacteristically dark here, even for deep space. Different crew members are taking readings of the surrounding area on their individual consoles. KIRK: "What have we got, Sulu?" SULU: "My sensors are not picking up anything out there…" SPOCK: "Captain, there seem to be some very unusual readings emanating from a confined area of space about 80,000 kilometers off of our port bow." KIRK: "What is it, Spock?" SPOCK: "Uncertain. It appears to be some sort of…disturbance in the fabric of space-time." KIRK: "A wormhole?" SPOCK: "It does not conform to the standard characteristics of what classic wormhole theory would predict. It is more like a—" SULU: "Captain! A ship has just appeared on our sensors on an intercept course." KIRK: "Can you identify it?" SULU: "All I know is that it is not a Federation ship." KIRK: "Yellow alert! Raise shields." A Tholian ship appears on the viewscreen. SULU: "They are hailing." KIRK: "Onscreen." Commander Loskene appears on their viewscreen. KIRK: "This is Captain Kirk of the United Federation of Planets—" LOSKENE: "I am Commander Loskene. You are trespassing in a territorial annex of the Tholian Assembly." KIRK: "I did not realize. We are on a peaceful mission investigating the disappearance of one of our ships—" LOSKENE: "If you do not leave immediately, you risk war upon you and your Federation." Kirk signals Sulu to cut off the sound. KIRK: "Sulu, what is the firepower of that ship?" SULU: "Insignificant compared to us. It is unlikely that it could have done anything to the Defiant." KIRK: "Spock, any other readings?" SPOCK: "Aside from the anomalous readings off of our port bow, there is nothing else out of the ordinary, and no residual energy signatures to indicate that any weapons have been fired or that any ship has been attacked here in the last seven days." Kirk motions for Sulu to turn on the sound. KIRK: "We apologize for trespassing in your space and will leave immediately. I would like to extend an invitation of friendship on behalf of the United Federation of Planets and hope that we may better get to know you and your people—" LOSKENE: "We will observe and see if you are true to your words of peace. If so, we may consider an alliance with you in the future." The transmission ends, and the Tholian ship departs. Kirk turns and looks at Sulu. KIRK: "Friendly bunch, weren't they?" SULU: "Very." KIRK: "Let's go home, Sulu." SULU: "Yes, sir."

~~~~~~~

The *Enterprise* is on its way back to Earth. McCoy enters the Bridge with a medical tricorder and starts scanning Kirk. KIRK: "Bones! Is there a problem?" MCCOY: "There was something funny about that region of space. Just doing some routine scans to make sure there is nothing out of the ordinary." Kirk walks over to Spock working at his console while McCoy follows him, scanning. McCoy starts scanning Spock as Kirk pats him on the back. KIRK: "Spock! Are you ready to explore all of the mysteries that lie waiting for us over the next five years?" Spock looks up from his work as Uhura flashes him another nasty look. McCoy catches it and looks at Spock. MCCOY: "Uh, oh, Spock...incoming photon torpedo." McCoy walks away from them, scanning others on the Bridge. UHURA: "Yes, *Spock*...why don't you tell him about how excited you are to join us on our five-year mission!" Spock turns towards Kirk, thinking that he is out of earshot of Uhura. SPOCK: "Captain, we need to talk." KIRK: "What is it, Spock?" SPOCK: "Can we go somewhere private?" KIRK: "Sure, of course we—" UHURA: "You can't tell him here? Why don't you want everyone on the Bridge to know that you're leaving Starfleet?" Everyone looks up from what they are doing, and McCoy stops his scanning. Kirk looks at Spock in stunned silence. KIRK: "Spock! Is it true? You're leaving???" SPOCK: "My race is an endangered species, Captain. Things are not going well on New Vulcan. They are lacking in...virile males to help repopulate—" UHURA: "So you have decided to jump into the stud services industry—or were you thinking of just becoming a gigolo instead? I hear that the right Vulcan male can fetch quite a high price these days..." Kirk slowly walks over to his chair and sits down as Spock follows. KIRK: "I understand your desire to help your people in any way that you can, but I was counting on you, Spock... How am I going to find a replacement this soon before our mission?" SPOCK: "There are many suitable replacements at your disposal: Hikaru Sulu, Montgomery Scott...or Lieutenant Uhura." Uhura flashes him the nastiest look yet. MCCOY (in Spock's ear): "Oh, no, my friend. That ain't going to get you out of the doghouse." KIRK: "Why didn't you tell me sooner, Spock?" SPOCK: "I only found out the true nature of things upon New Vulcan a few days ago and I tried—" UHURA: "You have never tried, Spock! It has always been about you and saving the Vulcan race! What about *us*? Doesn't that mean anything to you at all?" SPOCK: "You know it does, Nyota. But I have a duty to my people." UHURA: "Your people are here, Spock. Your duty is here. *I*...am here." SPOCK (after a pause): "The needs of the many outweigh the needs of the few. I am sorry, Nyota."

~~~~~~~

[Mirror universe, 22nd century, stardate 2156.4]
A torturer is turning knobs and pushing buttons as a captive Tholian makes high-pitched, irritating scratching noises in its native language. It is being held in an enclosed torture chamber, designed to mimic the extreme temperatures of its natural environment. As the torturer continues manipulating his control panel, a seductive, dark-haired woman, the Empress Hoshi Sato, enters the room, seen from behind. EMPRESS: "Has it revealed to us how they were able to create that wormhole into the other universe?" TORTURER: "No, Empress. It has proven itself very resistant to our extensive...*persuasions*." EMPRESS (addressing the Tholian): "Your species has been able to fight us off in the past, but now, with the new ship that we acquired with its 23rd century technology, you don't stand a chance. We have already wiped out most of the colonies on your home world, and if you don't cooperate, you will be the last of your kind." The Tholian makes some squeaky, scratching noises at her. EMPRESS: "That insult will cost you the death of the rest of your species!" The Tholian makes some louder, more

irritating scratching noises towards her. EMPRESS: "Maybe *this* will change your attitude…"

She nods to the torturer, and he brings in some more, smaller Tholians, being held in their own separate torture chambers. The first Tholian starts squealing its distress call. EMPRESS: "That won't help you…and soon your children will all be squealing if you don't give me what I want!"

[Normal universe, 23rd century]
The planet of New Vulcan is seen from space. It has none of the vibrant green and blue colors of earth, but is redder, closer to that of Mars. The perspective changes, zooming towards a large continent near the equator. As it gets closer, a small community is seen from above. There are no opulent buildings there, like there was on Vulcan, just humble dwellings that look like they are mostly made of the red clay that characterizes so much of the planet. The perspective moves to the front of a large building in the center of the community. There is a sign in the front of it that says, "Office of Vulcan Compatibility."

Spock is sitting inside a sparsely decorated office. Across a small, nondescript table sits Norbek, a young Vulcan woman with straight hair and only moderate looks. They are in the middle of a conversation. SPOCK: "I find it discomforting to be meeting you under these circumstances." NORBEK: "That is a human emotion we Vulcans do not have the luxury to indulge in these days." Spock looks slightly annoyed. SPOCK: "All I'm saying, Norbek, is that the circumstances are very unusual here. Normally I would be meeting you after both of our families have carefully considered as to whether we would be a prosperous and compatible match for each other." NORBEK: "As you may have noticed, most of us don't have our families, anymore. The Office of Compatibility is the most efficient way for Vulcans to meet each other now." There is an uncomfortable silence for a moment as the two of them regard each other from across the table. Then they both speak at the same time. NORBEK: "Maybe—" SPOCK: "I—" They both stop talking. SPOCK: "You speak first." NORBEK: "No, go ahead." SPOCK: "I would like to see you again." Norbek pauses for a moment before answering, with an indecipherable expression upon her face. NORBEK: "That would be…agreeable."

[Mirror universe, 22nd century]
We see an imposingly tall palace on the edge of a cliff looking out over the ocean, near to where Starfleet Headquarters would be if it were on the earth in the normal universe. It is well fortified with all sorts of futuristic weapons around it, designed to withstand any army. There are two towers that stand above everything else. The tallest one is where the Empress resides, while the second one, connected by a bridge to the first one, is flat on top, where the USS *Defiant* rests. The Empress is lounging upon her bed, with her trusted friend, Shaynil, comfortably sitting in a luxurious chair next to her. A female servant attentively stands nearby, ready to serve. EMPRESS (to the servant): "Leave us." The servant bows and quickly leaves the room. Shaynil sits more upright, sensing the Empress has something important to confide in her. SHAYNIL: "What is it, Empress?" After a moment, the Empress sits up and looks at her. EMPRESS: "I don't know who to trust, Shaynil. It feels like everyone around me is ready to stab a knife in my back in order to replace me." SHAYNIL: "No one would be able to succeed. You are a trained martial artist, and you have guards to protect you whenever you are in public. And then there's your ship—no one will dare challenge you with the most powerful ship in the Empire—" EMPRESS: "Little good it will do me if I have a knife in my back. If I am to maintain my power, I need to find a way to protect myself from an attack in any situation." SHAYNIL: "What do you have in mind?" EMPRESS: "I don't know." *(after a pause)* "The only thing I do know, is that if I can't defend myself anywhere—even in my very own bedroom—then I won't be here much longer."

~~~~~~~

[Normal universe, 23rd century]
We see the *Enterprise* docked at the Orbital Drydock Facility, close to Earth. Captain Kirk and Sulu are walking down a corridor. KIRK: "I have managed to pull some strings with Starfleet Academy to get acting Ensign Jaylah to take your place at the helm during our five-year mission into the Robidian Nebula..." They continue walking as Sulu listens. KIRK: "In addition to overseeing the Bridge crew, as first officer, you will be my greatest support—someone I can count on to give me feedback and a second opinion. It is your duty to tell me if and when you think I might be making a bad decision." SULU: "I understand, sir." KIRK (smiling): "Which will rarely—if ever—happen." Kirk and Sulu enter the Engineering Section of the ship. Scott is working at a console near the warp engines. KIRK: "Scotty! How's it going with the repairs?" SCOTT: "Capt'n, I don't know what it was about that region of space that we were in, but the warp nacelles are just not alignin'

properly." *(caressing the warp core)* "She's a wee-bit fussy of a lass, and somethin' back there just rubbed her the wrong way." KIRK: "How long will it take to finish the repairs, Scotty?" SCOTT: "I can't be sure. It could take a couple more weeks to get her purrin' properly again." KIRK: "We've already been delayed almost a month due to...*unforeseen circumstances*." He and Sulu exchange a look. KIRK: "We don't have a couple of weeks, Scotty." SCOTT: "Well, at least give me one more week to make sure everythin's workin' as best as she can. It would be a real shame to finally get out into that nebula, only to find out that the cylinders aren't all firin' properly."

[Mirror universe, 22nd century]
The same Tholian that was tortured before is in its altered torture chamber that now has mechanical arms protruding out of it. It is manipulating some device with a large circular ring in the center of it, similar to a miniature stargate. The Empress is in the room, observing what is happening. Sound frequencies shift, akin to tuning a radio receiver, but the sounds are much higher pitched.

While the Tholian manipulates the device with its mechanical arms, the space inside of the circular ring "warbles" and shifts; sometimes what looks like a tear or an opening in space-time appears for a split second and then quickly disappears again. At one point, while the Tholian is manipulating the device, a larger opening appears, revealing a being of bright white light inside of it. The Tholian begins emitting an alarm as it starts vigorously manipulating the device and the being of light disappears. EMPRESS: "What was that?!? Get it back immediately!!!" The Tholian keeps emitting its alarm while frantically moving levers and dials. EMPRESS: *"Get it back!!!"* More squealing. EMPRESS: "Get it back *now*, or you will be tortured for so long that you will wish you were dead!"

[Normal universe, 23rd century, New Vulcan housing complex]
We see many small domiciles from above before zooming down to where Spock is in his small apartment. There are very few furnishings inside, giving it a Spartan-like appearance. He is having dinner with Norbek. There is a very cold feel to the scene. SPOCK: "I have known you for three months now, Norbek, and I feel that we have been...harmonious together." Norbek does not say anything. SPOCK: "It is my hope that I will be able to contribute to the flourishing of the Vulcan race once again..." Norbek

continues to listen without saying anything. SPOCK: "I want to raise a family with you, Norbek." Norbek continues looking at him inscrutably with an emotionless expression upon her face. There is a moment of uncomfortable silence between them. NORBEK: "It is...agreeable to me."

Later that night, Spock and Norbek are making love together in Spock's bedroom. There is very little excitement in their actions, nor any noise. In the middle of their climax, as they are embracing each other, we see a close-up of Norbek with a bored and resigned look upon her face.

~~~~~~

[Mirror universe, 22nd century]
The scene changes from Norbek's emotionless face to the face of the Empress in the mirror universe, in sharp contrast to each other. Her face is somewhat obscured by her hair. She is in her concubine room, a dark room filled with all sorts of sexually themed devices. There are male and female humans, as well as other alien species in the room, all with electronic collars upon them. She is on top of one of the aliens, topless and with a whip in her hand, moving up and down with enthusiasm.

EMPRESS: "Yes! *Yes!! More!!!*" She cracks her whip and starts moving up and down even faster. EMPRESS: "*Oh, yes! Ohhhh, yesss, yesssss!*" After a moment, she starts to relax, and then looks down at the alien. EMPRESS (speaking in its language): "I have never known a species with such endurance. And with your legendary endowments, you truly are God's gift to women." She carefully climbs off of him, casually slips on her attire, and walks out the door.

~~~~~~

The Empress is walking down a corridor by herself, after leaving her concubine room. Four large men with weapons appear behind her from different side corridors as she walks by. One of them shoots at her, and a bubble force field (similar to the Borg) neutralizes the blast. She turns around and they run at her. She has a palm device that she points at two of them, vaporizing them instantly. The other two manage to get to her, swinging, one with a sword. Having a black belt in Aikido, she ducks the blows and knocks the one with the sword, Rasker, down to the ground with a side kick. As she does so, however, the other man grabs her from behind in a choke hold. She manages to push a button on her left wrist, and a flash occurs within her bubble shield that instantly vaporizes him.

At the same time, Rasker does a sweep kick that knocks her down and he pins her to the ground. RASKER: "Ha! Now I have you, *Empress*. I've got your arms pinned so you can't vaporize me." The Empress struggles to break free, but is unable to do so. Rasker continues to easily keep her pinned down. His sword is lying upon the floor out of reach, but a long, nasty-looking knife hangs in a scabbard around his waist. RASKER (sneering): "All of the little gadgets that those light beings designed for you—well, they're mine now." *(smiling maliciously)* "And when I become the new Emperor, people will fear me, and not dare to challenge me with all of your newfangled devices in my possession." *(laughing haughtily)* "But, first...before I kill you, maybe I will enjoy a little bit of the spoils..."

EMPRESS (cool and defiantly): "Do you really think that I have to push a button in order to vaporize you?" Rasker is thrown off a bit by her threat, but then he quickly regains his confidence. RASKER: "You're bluffing. You're just a weak woman who doesn't deserve to rule over the Empire. We need a man who is stronger and more powerful than you." She continues to struggle helplessly under his weight. EMPRESS: "You are right about one thing: You are stronger...but I am smarter." (forcefully) *"Hish'tanga!!!"*

Another flash occurs within her bubble force field, vaporizing Rasker immediately. The only thing that remains of him is his long, nasty-looking knife, which clangs to the floor noisily. The Empress gets up and continues walking down the corridor in the same direction as if nothing happened, leaving the sword and the knife upon the floor.

~~~~~~

The Empress enters a room where a cylindrical device, about four-feet tall, is pulsating with a faint aura around it. A scientist in the room is inspecting it and taking readings. EMPRESS: "Is it working?" SCIENTIST: "As far as I can tell, Empress. We have made it to their exact specifications and followed their instructions precisely on the activation procedure." EMPRESS: "Can you tell what it's supposed to do?" SCIENTIST: "We have no idea. The design of this device is unlike anything that we have ever seen before." EMPRESS (eyeing it critically): "Do you think it is safe to launch?" SCIENTIST: "The only thing that we have been able to detect with this device is a very slight distortion in the fabric of space-time. It seems localized to a very small space around the device itself. As far as I can tell, it is not having any effect on anything outside of that area—" EMPRESS: "As far as you can *tell!?* So you don't know for sure?" SCIENTIST (nervous):

"Begging your pardon, Empress, but this device is using a technology that we have never seen before, so we can't be sure of anything regarding as to what its purpose is, or why those beings of light want you to build them..."

[Normal universe, 23rd century]
Spock and his fiancé are having dinner together in his small apartment on New Vulcan. There is a strained formalness to their interactions. Very little conversation is happening between the two of them, and the young Vulcan woman seems even more reserved than usual. SPOCK: "Is everything all right, Norbek?" Norbek doesn't respond and continues to peck at her food. SPOCK: "Are you regretting the decision to marry me?" NORBEK: "Vulcans are not capable of having regrets." Norbek continues pecking at her food, and then looks up at Spock. NORBEK: "There has been...talk among some of the other Vulcans in the community. SPOCK (restrained anger): "Talk? What kind of talk?" Norbek looks away and does not speak. SPOCK: "Tell me, Norbek, what kind of talk?" Norbek looks back down, pecking at her food. NORBEK: "They have been saying that you shouldn't be here...that only pure-blooded Vulcans should be here to rebuild our race so that our children are not tainted—" SPOCK (annoyed): "Tainted? They think I am here to...*taint* our race?" Norbek pecks at her food and does not respond. SPOCK: "Who are these *pure*-blooded Vulcans that are saying this?" Norbek looks up at Spock, but does not say anything. SPOCK: "What about you, Norbek? Do you agree with them?" Norbek looks at Spock for a moment, and then looks down. SPOCK: "Answer me, Norbek. Do you believe what they are saying?" Norbek looks up from her food and into Spock's eyes. NORBEK: "I don't know what to believe, anymore."

[Normal universe, 23rd century]
The *Enterprise* is approaching the Robidian Nebula, a massive, multicolored nebula spanning across thousands of light years. Kirk is in the captain's chair, with Sulu to his right, and Jaylah at the helm. JAYLAH: "Where to, Captain?" KIRK: "Straight ahead, and then make a turn towards the first mysterious anomaly that we see, Jaylah..." JAYLAH: "Yes, sir."

We see the *Enterprise* enter into the nebula and disappear.

Sometime later, we see the *Enterprise* approaching an anomalous blinking star inside of the nebula, shown on the viewscreen. KIRK: "What is it, Sulu?" SULU (looking at his console): "I don't know, Captain." KIRK: "Take her in a little closer, Jaylah, so we can get some readings." JAYLAH: "Yes, sir—" UHURA: "Captain, I am receiving an audio distress call from an unidentified ship. It is faint and breaking up..." KIRK: "Put it on." We hear the distress call over the com *(faint and crackling)*: "This is the USS Robert Fox. We are caught in some sort of energy ribbon and are unable to escape. Gravimetric distortions are buckling our hull. We do not know how long we will be able to—" UHURA: "I lost the signal, sir!" KIRK: "Can you pinpoint its location?" UHURA: "About two light years from here...outside of the nebula. KIRK (after a momentary pause): "Take us out of here, Jaylah, maximum warp."

~~~~~~

The *Enterprise* arrives at the location of the distress call. There are two ships there: the USS *Robert Fox* and the *Lakul*, both partially caught in the Nexus. SULU: "The hull integrity of the Robert Fox is critical. Collapse is imminent!" KIRK: "Lock onto her with a tractor beam, Sulu." Sulu works his console and a tractor beam from the *Enterprise* locks onto the ship and begins to pull it out. Just as the ship is almost free, a massive discharge erupts from the Nexus, destroying the *Robert Fox* and then follows up the tractor beam, hitting the *Enterprise*. SULU: "We've lost the Robert Fox! A resonance burst from the Nexus knocked out our primary systems. We are running on auxiliary power only." KIRK: "How many lives on board the Robert Fox?" SULU: "265 souls, sir." On the viewscreen, a small explosion occurs on the right wing of the *Lakul*. SULU: "The Lakul is critical! Forty-five seconds before hull collapse!" KIRK: "Take her in to within transporter range, Jaylah." SULU: "Sir, our hull integrity has already been weakened by that last discharge. We may not be able to handle the gravimetric distortions at that range." KIRK: "Take her in, Jaylah." JAYLAH: "Yes, sir." The *Enterprise* slowly approaches the *Lakul*. SULU: "Twenty seconds before collapse!" KIRK (hitting his combadge): "Scotty, transport all of the passengers of the Lakul directly to Sickbay." SCOTT (over the com): "Aye, Capt'n!" Gravimetric distortions are rocking the *Enterprise* as Scott starts beaming the El-Aurians on board. A moment later, the *Lakul* explodes. KIRK: "Status, Mr. Scott!" SCOTT: "I was only able to get 46 out of 150, Capt'n." Kirk slumps in his chair. The gravimetric distortions increase as the Nexus continues to approach the *Enterprise*. KIRK: "Get us out of here, Jaylah. Full reverse!" JAYLAH: "The helm's not responding, Captain!" The

Enterprise begins shaking violently. KIRK: "Give it all she's got, Jaylah!" The engines of the *Enterprise* are heard whining as it tries to escape the gravitational distortions of the Nexus. SCOTT (over the com): "Capt'n! The engines will tear the Enterprise apart in these gravimetric distortions." KIRK: "Any suggestions, Mr. Scott?" SCOTT: "An anti-matter discharge might disrupt the field long enough for us to break away." KIRK: "Sulu, can you launch a photon torpedo?" SULU: "The weapons system was taken out from that last discharge that hit us." SCOTT: "You might be able to simulate a torpedo blast using a resonance burst from the main deflector dish, Capt'n." SULU: "It would require making the necessary modifications for it work." Kirk jumps out of his chair as the ship continues to be rocked around. KIRK: "You have the Bridge, Sulu." SULU: "Captain, you should be here! Let me go." Kirk is walking towards the door. KIRK (as the door closes): "No time."

~~~~~~~

We see Kirk in the main deflector room. He rips off a large wall panel and starts furiously pulling and re-inserting cables and data modules as the ship continues to shake and shudder. The scene flips back to the Bridge, where we see Sulu in the captain's chair while another officer has replaced him at his console. The ship is shaking badly. OFFICER: "Thirty-five seconds to structural collapse!" Meanwhile, in the main deflector room, Kirk continues to work furiously, moving things around. SCOTT (over the com): "Capt'n, I don't know how much longer I can hold her together!" Kirk finally finishes and slams the wall panel shut. KIRK: "That should do it. Let's get out of here, Sulu!" SULU (in the captain's chair): "Activate the main deflector!" The officer works her console…

We see the *Enterprise* out in space. A large burst of energy leaps out of the main deflector dish and explodes in front of the ship. The Nexus roils and fluctuates in response as the *Enterprise* starts to move away from it.

OFFICER (looking at his console in the Bridge): "We're breaking free, sir…" *(after a pause)* "Kirk did it!"

As the *Enterprise* continues to move further away from the Nexus, in parallel with what happened to Kirk in the prime universe, an arcing band of energy bursts out of it and hits the lower decks of the ship, tearing a hole in it as the ship moves further away from the Nexus and into safety.

The scene reverts back to the Bridge. The ship is hit so hard that everyone is knocked down. Gradually, the shaking stops, and everything becomes calm. SULU (climbing back into his chair): "Report!" OFFICER: "There is a hull breach in the lower part of the ship. Emergency force fields are in place and holding..." SULU (face turning pale): "Which sections?" OFFICER: "Sections 20 through 28 on Decks 13...14..." (he looks up at Sulu) "...and 15." SULU: "Bridge to Captain Kirk!" *(silence)* "Captain Kirk, please respond!" *(more silence)* "Mr. Scott, meet me on Deck 15!" Sulu leaps out of the captain's chair and runs out the door of the Bridge.

Sulu is running down a corridor, turns a corner, and then stops short. It looks out into empty space. The only thing keeping him from being sucked out is a flickering force field surrounded by jagged metal. Scott runs up to him from around the corner, out of breath. His jaw drops as he slowly looks at Sulu. SCOTT: "May the saints have mercy..."

We see the ship from outer space. As it slowly and peacefully drifts past, a huge chunk is seen missing from the lower part of it. The two small figures of Sulu and Scott can be seen standing in an open corridor, looking out into space.

[The Nexus]
Young Kirk is lying upon what looks like a dark granite bed. Only his face is seen. He opens his eyes, squinting, and with a grimace, he groans. KIRK (to himself): "Oooooh...I feel like I had 22 tequila shots too many." He sits up and looks around. Everything is blurry. He sees what seem to be indistinct oblong objects nearby. KIRK: "Where am I...?" WOMAN'S VOICE: "You're in heaven, Jim." He looks in the direction of the voice, and one of the oblong objects forms into his mother, Winona Kirk. KIRK: "Mother...!?" She looks at him, smiling, and puts her hands upon his cheeks. MOTHER: "My beautiful boy, you've finally come back." Kirk jumps off of the bed, which has subtly changed from a dark granite one into a normal, comfortable one with pillows. KIRK: "This can't be real. Just a second ago, I was on the Enterprise...I had just fixed...that was it! I had just modified the deflector array, and—" MAN'S VOICE: "—and then an arm of the Nexus hit that part of the ship you were in." Kirk sees another blurry oblong object near him come into view, turning into Christopher Pike. KIRK: "Admiral!? Is that really you?!?" PIKE: "It is, Jim." KIRK: "Am I really...dead?" Pike looks

at him with compassion. PIKE: "The moment the Nexus hit your ship, you died." Kirk is taken aback for a moment. KIRK: "And what about my crew?" PIKE: "What you did allowed them to break free from the Nexus. You saved them, Jim." Kirk walks away from Pike. KIRK (to himself): "This isn't right...it can't be true...I can't be dead!" FATHER'S VOICE: "You are...son."

As young Kirk looks at the blurry oblong object that spoke, it turns into his father, George Kirk. KIRK (stunned): "Father...!?" FATHER: "My son, I have waited for this moment for so long..." As he speaks, the room they are in takes on a warm, cozy feeling, with an orange glow to it. FATHER: "I have waited so long to tell you how much I love you..." A soft, white light begins to form behind him, subtly at first, and seemingly off in the distance. FATHER: "...and to tell you how proud I am of you." The light becomes brighter. Kirk's mother, his father, and Pike are looking at him with kind and loving smiles upon their faces. KIRK (pointing towards the light): "What is that?" FATHER: "It's where we live, son... It's time to come home."

[Normal universe, 23rd century]
A memorial service is being held for Kirk. The large auditorium is packed to overflowing with people, including most of the admirals and captains in Starfleet, who are sitting towards the back of the stage, behind a podium with Kirk's picture in front of it. All of the *Enterprise* crew is there, sitting in the front row.

Spock, in uniform, approaches the podium. As the large audience looks at him expectantly, he stands there for a moment, looking around, without speaking. SPOCK: "I was asked to come up here...to say something about James Tiberias Kirk...but words fail me." He pauses, continuing to look at everybody. SPOCK: "There are no words that can accurately attest to the true integrity of his character... He was honest, genuine, caring...and the best friend that I could have ever hoped to have had. He always followed his gut feelings and was irritatingly illogical at times..." (Mild laughter from the audience.) SPOCK: "...but it was that part of him that has helped me to appreciate and to accept the human part of who I am that has always seemed so foreign to me." Spock starts to get choked up as he stands there, struggling with his emotions. Then, a single tear starts to roll down his cheek. SPOCK (faltering): "I have become a better person from knowing him..." His voice trails off as one of the admirals at the back of the stage stands up and blows a boatswain's whistle. Everyone in the auditorium stands up as one person in silent attention for sixty seconds.

~~~~~

Most of the admirals and captains are eating and drinking and having soft conversations in small groups in a nearby reception room. The crew of the *Enterprise* is also there, quietly milling about. Spock is standing by himself, away from the different conversations, with a drink in his hand. Uhura, on the other side of the room, gives him a somewhat angry glance. McCoy comes up to Spock, pats him on the shoulder, and raises his glass. MCCOY: "To the greatest man we have ever known." They touch glasses and take a drink. MCCOY (congenially): "I remember once when I was stuck with him in a—" Spock catches another angry glance from Uhura. SPOCK: If you'll excuse me, Doctor, there is something that I need to attend to..." McCoy looks in the direction Spock is looking to catch one of Uhura's angry glances. MCCOY: "Oh—right. Be careful with that one...I don't want the Enterprise crew to suffer two casualties in one week."

Spock slowly makes his way across the room towards Uhura, occasionally stopping to exchange trite words with people he bumps into along the way. As he gets closer, Uhura starts to walk away. SPOCK: "Nyota..." Uhura turns towards him with a mixture of sorrow and anger. UHURA: "What is it, Spock?" SPOCK (short pause): "I'm sorry." Uhura glares at him. UHURA: "You're sorry." Spock stands there for a moment, unsure of what to say next. SPOCK: "Starfleet has granted me permission to continue on with Kirk's five-year mission into the Robidian Nebula, as captain of the Enterprise." Uhura turns and looks at him with a mixture of surprise and anger. UHURA: "What about your wife—what's her name? *Norbok?* Won't she miss you?" SPOCK: "I broke off my engagement with Norbek." *(restrained anger)* "I won't be raising a family upon New Vulcan, anymore." UHURA: "So you messed up that relationship too, huh, Spock?" Spock looks away and doesn't say anything for a moment. SPOCK: "If my presence would make you uncomfortable in any way, I will ask that my commission be reassigned to another ship..." Uhura smiles facetiously and blinks. UHURA (falsetto): "Why would you make me uncomfortable?"

~~~~~

[Mirror universe, 22nd century]
The Empress, seen from behind, is communicating with what looks like a ghostly, holographic being of bright, white light. He starts to fade out within

the large, central ring of the device in the center of the room. EMPRESS (yelling): "*Don't let him fade!!!*" The Tholian in the modified torture chamber with the protruding mechanical arms manipulates some dials and levers on the holographic device. Some sound frequencies shift, and the hologram becomes more stable. Using a hand-held translation device, she starts to have a dialogue with the being of light. An eerie, staccato noise between a slur and a hiss is heard coming from the holographic image in the central ring of the device. She looks at her translator, and then looks up at it. EMPRESS (annoyed): "The only stable wormhole that the Tholians have been able to create connects to the other universe 108 years in the future. Even with the recent acquisition, our other ships will be no match against them. The enhanced shield technology you gave us will be helpful, but it is not enough... *I need more firepower.*"

More eerie noises come from the holographic image as the Empress looks at her translator. EMPRESS: "I have been fulfilling your request, creating the devices exactly as you specified. I have already placed many of them in orbit around different inhabited planets. I will continue to build them, but I will not activate one more until you give me the final piece of information that you promised me." The being of light moves out of view for a moment, and more of the eerie noises can be heard, more distant, and as if from different sources. The being comes back in view, along with two others behind it. The original one makes some more noises, and the Empress reads what it says on her translator. EMPRESS (excited): "Bring in the holoimager!" A large machine is wheeled in near her and is connected to a very large plug. EMPRESS (eagerly): "It is ready." After a short pause, all three beings of light start to make complex slurring and hissing noises, and as they do so, the machine starts translating the noises into an intricate three-dimensional holographic schematic for what looks to be an ultra-powerful weapon. As the Empress watches the design unfolding on the machine in front of her, her eyes glisten with anticipation.

[Normal universe, 23rd century]
It has been five years since Captain Kirk's death, and the *Enterprise* is leaving the Robidian Nebula, on its way home. It looks battered, like it has been through more than it can handle. SPOCK'S VOICE: "Captain's log, stardate 2269.5..." Spock is seen walking down a corridor, passing different crew members. SPOCK'S VOICE: "We have just completed our five-year mission into the Robidian Nebula and are on our way back to Earth. We have had

more than our fair share of challenges, from encountering a vast field of micro-asteroids that were actually metal-ingesting space organisms..." The hull of the *Enterprise* is seen being devoured by voracious, rock-like creatures. SPOCK'S VOICE: "...to having the warp core almost completely drained by cloaked hostile alien ships to the point of compromising life-support systems..." Crew members are seen falling down and gasping for air. SPOCK'S VOICE: "...to getting caught in the middle of an anticyclonic super storm in the atmosphere of a gas giant, deactivating our navigational systems for most of a day..." The *Enterprise* is seen swirling around and around in a giant atmospheric storm similar to Jupiter's Great Red Spot. SPOCK'S VOICE: "...but overall, the crew has shown exemplary ingenuity and adaptability to all of the challenges that they have gone through, and have managed to work well with each other despite all of the hardships that they have faced being together on this ship for such a long period of time..." A crew member is seen strangling another one. A man in boxers is seen leaving a woman's quarters as she throws his pants in the corridor behind him. The *Enterprise* is seen continuing on its way home, looking as ragged as ever. SPOCK'S VOICE: "...I believe that we have grown from all of the challenges that we have faced together..." Spock is seen walking down the same corridor as in the earlier scene. Only this time, every crew member turns after he passes and looks at him with loathing. SPOCK'S VOICE: "...and that we are all truly grateful to have completed the late Captain Kirk's final mission to its very end."

~~~~~~

[Normal universe, 24th century, stardate 2381.8]
Picard is sitting in a cushioned chair in his living room with his legs femininely crossed, sipping tea. There is a similar chair across from him, but he is alone. Suddenly, Q is sitting in the other chair, legs crossed in similar fashion, looking as cool as can be. As Picard looks up, he sees him and jumps up, spilling his tea. PICARD: "Q! What are you doing here?!? I had hoped that I would never—" Q: "I know, I know. Here I am again, Picard, because something terrible is about to happen to the universe, and who is it that always comes to save the day...but your old friend, Q." PICARD: "This is really getting old, Q—" Q: "*I'm* getting old, Picard...old and tired of always being humanity's cosmic babysitter—right there, always ready to lend a helping hand whenever something goes wrong. And do I ever hear even one tiny, little, teensy-weensy 'thank you' for all of these selfless acts of generosity? You know, one of these days, I won't be here for humanity anymore, and then what will you do?" PICARD: "Enough, Q! I don't have

time for your games. Just get to the point!" Q: "The point, Picard, is that something terrible is about to happen to your universe, and if you don't do something about it, I won't be to blame, as I have done my duty in warning you." PICARD: "If it is about the Cardassians and their secret inter-dimensional weapon that they are building in the Neutral Zone, we can handle it ourselves, thank you very much." Q: "Will you ever start thinking beyond the two dimensions right in front of your face, Picard? If there was one thing that I had hoped that you would have gotten from all of your adventures with me, it is that the universe isn't as flat and boring as your puny, single-celled mind imagines it to be. No, something terrible is about to happen 112 years ago that will change the fate of your *grandiose* Federation, and the universe as you know it." PICARD: "112 years ago…and it is about to happen now? Don't waste my time with your riddles, Q!" Q snaps his fingers, and they are in the middle of space, except it is filled with what looks like flowing rivers of energy everywhere. Q: "This is not a riddle, Picard…this is the fate of your universe." PICARD: "Where have you taken me, Q?!? What shenanigans are you playing me for this time?" Q: "I haven't taken you anywhere, Picard. We are, here, in your living room—or what used to be your living room—283 years in the future. What your Federation calls the Nexus is about to consume your entire universe, and when that happens, not a single living creature will exist in it anymore." Q pauses for a moment with an exaggerated, wide-eyed, expectant look upon his face. Q: "Wait for it…" PICARD: "The Federation has been aware of the Nexus since the disappearance of Captain Kirk. It has not increased in any significant amount since we began monitoring it 117 years ago!" Q: "Boop! There it is. The universe has just been completely consumed by the Nexus and is lost forever." The Nexus is everywhere all around them and looks exactly the same as it did a moment earlier. PICARD: "I am done playing your games. Take me back, Q!" Q snaps his fingers, and they are back in Picard's living room. PICARD: "I am not going on anymore of your adventures, Q. The universe can and will survive just fine without you! Leave, and do not ask for my help, ever again." Q: "As you wish, mon capitaine. It is now out of my hands. The fate of the universe rests with you, Picard." Q snaps his fingers and disappears.

~~~~~~

[Normal universe, 23rd century]
The USS *Excelsior* is exploring the region of space where the USS *Defiant* had disappeared five years earlier. Various members of the *Excelsior* crew are on different consoles, including Lieutenant Jorger, making scans. Captain

Usean is studying the pitch black viewscreen from his chair. JORGER: "It is nice of the Tholians to allow us to finally take in-depth scans of this area." USEAN: "It's been five years, Jorger. It might be too late to ever figure out what has happened to the Defiant. There seems to be absolutely nothing out there..." The region of space shown on the viewscreen starts warbling. JORGER: "Sir, I am starting to pick up some very unusual readings..." USEAN: "What is it, Lieutenant?" Suddenly, a massive wormhole appears on the viewscreen. USEAN: "Red alert! Raise shields." USEAN (to Jorger): "Is that what I think it is?" JORGER: "Affirmative, Captain. I am looking at my readings, and I still can't believe it." USEAN: "Believe what, Jorger?" JORGER: "If these readings are accurate, this is the first stable, bidirectional wormhole that has ever been encountered. Its properties conform exactly to what Chandrasekhar predicted it would have. This could finally end centuries of vehement debate among leading scientists on this subject." USEAN: "Chandrasekhar? Wasn't he the one who calculated the limit of how large the mass of a star could be and still resist gravitational collapse?" JORGER: "That was *Subrahmanyan* Chandrasekhar. It was his great-great-granddaughter, Riya, who proposed her theory 98 years after—" Jorger stops in mid-sentence. USEAN: "What is it, Jorger?" JORGER: "Sir, there appears to be something coming out of the wormhole." On the viewscreen, a fuzzy object is seen moving from out of the wormhole. As it leaves its event horizon, it clarifies into the USS *Defiant*, looking in perfect condition. JORGER: "Sir...it's the Defiant!" USEAN: "I can't believe it! Hail them!" There is no response. USEAN: "This is Captain Usean of the USS Excelsior. Captain Shaw, are you there, old friend? What a sight for sore eyes! We thought we had lost you and your ship for good." On their viewscreen appears a malicious-looking man in a Terran uniform. ZERTHOS: "I am Captain Zerthos of the Terran Empire. Captain Shaw is dead...and so are you."

The viewscreen cuts off, and the USS *Defiant* fires upon the *Excelsior*. Its lasers go right through their shields, crippling it. More lasers are shot, crippling it even more. USEAN: "Send out an emergency distress signal to Starfleet! This is Captain Usean of the USS Excelsior. We are under attack by some alien species that has taken over the USS Defiant. They claim they are part of what they call the Terran Empire. We need immediate backup! I do not know how long—"

The USS *Defiant* fires another shot, and the USS *Excelsior* explodes.

The *Enterprise* is passing Yorktown Starbase, on their way home towards Earth. SULU: "Captain, incoming signal from Commadore Paris." SPOCK: "Onscreen." Commadore Paris appears on the viewscreen. SPOCK: "Commadore." PARIS (grim-faced): "Captain Spock, the USS Excelsior has been destroyed by an alien race that has taken over the USS Defiant in Tholian space. You have been ordered by Central Command to rendezvous with the rest of Starfleet to assess and to neutralize the current threat. Your homecoming, which is so well deserved by you and all of your crew, is going to have to wait." SPOCK: "Duty comes first, Commadore. We will alter course immediately." There are noticeable looks of frustration on the faces of different crew members. PARIS: "Godspeed." The viewscreen goes blank. SPOCK: "Jaylah, set a new course heading for Tholian space, maximum warp."

~~~~~

The *Enterprise,* still in its dilapidated state, jumps out of warp, appearing at the wormhole where the USS *Defiant* awaits in front of it. There are already other Starfleet vessels there when the *Enterprise* arrives, and more ships are seen appearing after it. SPOCK: "Hail the Defiant, Sulu." Captain Zerthos appears on the viewscreen. SPOCK: "This is Captain Spock of the flagship USS Enterpr—" ZERTHOS: "If you and your fleet surrender at once, we will show you mercy—at least as much mercy as a weak subspecies such as yourselves deserve—" SPOCK: "We will never surrender!" He turns to Sulu. SPOCK: "Fire upon that ship with everything we've got." The USS *Defiant* is fired upon, and it causes no damage. ZERTHOS (still onscreen): "Such a waste of good firepower. Oh, well...one can only hope." Zerthos turns to an officer. ZERTHOS: "Bring in the fleet." The viewscreen goes blank. SULU: "Captain, I am seeing 5...no wait...16...no...37 more ships appearing from out of the wormhole." SPOCK: "Onscreen." The viewscreen shows 37 ships that look like upgrades of the Federation's ships.

A massive battle ensues between the two fleets. The Terran ships destroy the Federation ships quickly and without any damage to themselves. The USS *Enterprise* is the last crippled ship remaining, and the firing stops. Out of the wormhole appears a larger, more advanced-looking ship than the other ones. Spock is sitting in the captain's chair watching it come out on the viewscreen, on the fritz, but still working. His hair is ruffled, and a large, green gash streaks across the right side of his face. The Bridge is in shambles. There is smoke everywhere, and there are dead crew members lying upon the floor, including Jaylah. The Empress appears on the viewscreen. EMPRESS:

"Flagship *Enterprise*, surrender your vess—" SPOCK: "You have committed an act of war against the Federation, and you will pay for your—" EMPRESS: "The Federation no longer exists. You are now part of the *United Terran Empire*...and you shall address me as *Empress Hoshi Sato*."

There are parts and shambles of Starfleet ships floating around everywhere as the Terran fleet sits calmly poised in front of the wormhole. The *Enterprise* has large holes in it and is venting plasma. The Empress' ship fires upon the *Enterprise*, and it explodes, flinging different pieces of it out in all directions. As the wreckage dissipates, we see a person, stiff and frozen, slowly rotating towards us in space. As it approaches, a close up of Spock's face rotates into view. His eyes are wide open, and there is a vacant expression upon his face. Then he drifts on by and is gone.

~~~~~~

[Normal universe, 24th century]
Picard is sitting in his Ready Room in his normal Starfleet uniform. As he sits there, it suddenly transforms: His uniform switches to that of the Terran Empire. His face becomes sharper and more scarred and strained. The items around the room and the wall decorations change to a more violent theme.

A secure-channel communication request appears on the monitor on his desk. Retired Admiral Pavel Chekov appears on the viewscreen. He looks extremely old and is bent over. Even though he is in the privacy of his Ready Room, Picard quickly looks around when he appears. PICARD (whispering): "Are you sure this channel is secure?" CHEKOV: "Trust me, Captain. I was risking my life in covert spy missions deep inside the Klingon Empire while you were still in holo-diapers—" PICARD: "Actually, my father believed in doing things the old-fashioned way and did not rely on replicator technology clean up my messes—" CHEKOV: "The point is, Captain, I became involved with Starfleet over 120 years ago, and being the leader of the Federation Alliance, I have learned a thing or two about making sure the two-bit spies of the Empire cannot eavesdrop into my conversations." PICARD: "Of course, Admiral. Just can never be too cautious. It seems like Terran spies lurk around every corner these days, just waiting for me to make some sort of slip so they can throw me into a torture chamber." CHEKOV: "I am almost 140 years old, Captain. Even with all of the newfangled technology that the Empire has, no one in recorded history has ever hit that mark before, and I intend to be the first one to do it. Do you know what my secret is?" PICARD: "Tell me." CHEKOV: "To not waste my energies on fearful thinking. Every day, when I wake up, I give my thanks for yet another gift that the universe has given to me. When my time comes, I will be grateful for everything that I have experienced, and will be ready to embark upon a new adventure." PICARD: "Well, I am sure that you will have many more gifts ahead of you before that time comes."

At that moment, Chekov's great-great-granddaughter, Nikita Tolstoy, appears on the viewscreen next to him. NIKITA: "It is time for your hydrotherapy session, Poppy." CHEKOV: "Have you met my great-great-granddaughter? She has been such a great help to me over the last few years." PICARD (smiling kindly): "Yes, we've met before. How are you, Nikita?" NIKITA: "I am well, but I wish my dear praskchur here would not be so involved with this rebellion." CHEKOV: "Hush! Let an old man have his fantasies. It is what keeps me alive. But, we should get on with business, Captain." CHEKOV (turning to Nikita): "Give us a few more minutes, pravnuchka. I will be done shortly." Nikita leaves from the viewscreen. CHEKOV: "Have you taken the readings?" PICARD (grim): "Yes. It is far worse than I imagined. The Nexus is much larger than expected." CHEKOV: "I knew it! I knew they were covering this up... Do you think it is the wormhole that is causing it? The Nexus wasn't expanding at all before the Empress opened it up into our universe over a century ago." PICARD: "I don't see how." *(pause)* "All I know is that if it continues to increase in size, it could become a real threat to both of our universes." CHEKOV (in a low tone): "You know what will happen to you if you report that—especially to one of us *lowly* humans." PICARD: "You needn't worry. This won't be the first time that I will have to lie on a report in order to save my own skin." Chekov sits back and thinks for a little bit. CHEKOV: "If word got out that they were keeping this from the people...it could really help our cause..." PICARD" I have got to do some final...*readings* before I leave this space. I will let you know everything that I discover, Admiral." Chekov crosses his hands, palms against his chest. CHEKOV (resolutely): "May the Federation Alliance prevail!" Picard quickly glances around his Ready Room, and then looks back at Chekov. He slowly places his hands across his chest, and quickly speaks in a low and quiet voice. PICARD: "May the Federation Alliance prevail."

~~~~~~

Picard enters the Bridge from his Ready Room. It looks like an improved version of the Bridge of the *Enterprise-E*, but it is darker in theme and lighting. The Terran symbol of the Empire is prominently displayed on the front of the most forward console. On the main viewscreen, the Nexus is seen, larger than ever, rippling through space as they follow alongside it from a safe distance.

A darkly uniformed Data approaches Picard and pulls him aside. DATA: "The Nexus has increased 17.39 times in size over the last 112 years, and it is increasing exponentially. I calculate that within 425 years, if left unchecked, it could consume the entire universe as we know it." PICARD: "Well, at least I won't have to worry about it, then." DATA: "But *I*…probably will." PICARD: "Do you have any theories as to how it might be growing?" DATA: "Absolutely none. This anomaly defies all laws of physics, and yet it is undeniably there, and getting larger every day." PICARD (lowering his voice): "Well, Data, I would suggest keeping all of this information to yourself, or some Terran official might decide that you need to go back to the reprogramming chamber." A dark look crosses Data's face. DATA: "I understand, sir."

As Data goes back to his console, Deanna Troi approaches Picard, her face ashen white. PICARD: "Counselor! Are you all right?" TROI: "Captain, can we talk?" PICARD: "Of course. Come into my Ready Room." Picard enters his Ready Room with Troi. TROI: "Jean-Luc, you are one of the only people who knows about my telepathic abilities—" PICARD: "And I would never betray your confidence, Deanna. I know that the Empire would turn you into a ruthless weapon with your capabilities. Whatever is going on...you can trust me." TROI: "There is something terribly wrong about the Nexus." The look in her eyes conveys both shock and fear. TROI: "I can sense...people in it." PICARD: "How could that be?" TROI: "I don't know...but I can feel them...I can feel more of them than I have ever felt before...more than there are people on the entire earth. Something is not right about them. It's like they are—" She looks completely overwhelmed, like a deer in headlights, and in the next moment, she starts to faint. PICARD (catching her): "Activate the Emergency Medical Hologram!"

A sinister-looking version of Voyager's EMH materializes in Picard's Ready Room. He is attired in the darkened uniform of the Terran Empire, busily working on his tricorder a few feet away. EMH (not looking up, annoyed): "This had better be a medical emergency! I am in the middle of some very *interesting* experiments with orangutans trying to amplify the pain signals in their brains through neuromagnetic stimulation…" He continues working on his tricorder as Troi, still in Picard's arms, begins to open her eyes. The EMH finally looks up and nonchalantly walks over to them as Troi begins to stand back upon her feet again. EMH: "Feeling a little *woozy*, are we?" The EMH starts using his tricorder to take readings of Picard. PICARD: "I'm not the one who is sick, Doctor." *(pointing to Troi)* "She is!" EMH (continuing to scan Picard): "Elevated heart rate...increased cortisol levels... You two must have been talking about something very interesting before I appeared..." *(looking suspiciously at them both)* "Nothing the emperor would disapprove of, *I'm sure*." TROI: "Computer, deactivate EMH!" EMH: "Fortunately, you can't deactivate me. After having a recent talk with the emperor himself about how to make his empire more *secure*, I am free to go wherever I want...*whenever* I want." *(giving them both a slow and menacing look)* "Let us pray that neither of you have a *real* medical emergency anytime soon." The EMH disappears from the room.

TROI: "I have never liked that computer program, even though they say he is better than any human doctor." PICARD: "We both know the reason Beverly was replaced is because they don't think we humans are worth the extra expense of having a *real* doctor." He starts to walk her towards the door. PICARD: "Ever since the Terrans modified Doctor Zimmerman's work, they have become more like spies than anything that is actually useful in any way." As the doors open to the Bridge, Data sees Troi being supported by Picard, and approaches them. DATA: "Is everything OK, Counselor?" TROI: "I'm fine, Data—just a little light-headed, that's all." PICARD: "Data, would you escort Deanna to her quarters?" DATA: "Absolutely, sir." They start to walk away. PICARD: "And Data..." DATA: "Yes, sir?" PICARD: "Let me know as soon as you have finished all of your readings. I want to get out of this place as soon as possible." DATA: "Yes, sir." Picard watches them walking away as the doors to his Ready Room close in front of him.

Q'S VOICE: "The Nexus is more nefarious and dangerous than even what your pet telepath senses, Picard." Pulling out his phaser, Picard whips around and points it at Q, who is sitting behind his desk with a mock-serious expression upon his face. He is wearing an exaggerated, funky Terran Empire uniform filled with all kinds of poufy baubles and medals. Q: "A little jumpy, aren't we, Picard? I must say...the Terran Empire has been just *dreadful* for your complexion!" PICARD (hitting his com badge): "Security!" Q: "Picard, is that any way to greet an old friend? Oh, that's right, your puny hominid brain can't remember anything beyond the pitiful universe that you see right in front of you." Picard (his face red): "Who are you!?" Q (dramatically): "My name is...*Q!*" PICARD: "I do not know anyone by that name! SECURITY!!!" Q: "Your little communication device won't help you...nor will your little toy ray gun." Picard looks down to see an overly large, plastic toy phaser in his hands. Q: "Come, sit down, Picard! Tea?" Suddenly, Picard is sitting with Q in a cute, outdoor French café on a beautiful sunny day. They are both in floofy French clothing. A gigantic cup of steaming hot tea sits in front of Picard. Q: "It's Earl Grey...just the way you like it!" PICARD (defensively looking around): "What is this? Have you drugged me? Am I in an interrogation chamber being tested right now? *I am not a secret rebel of the Federation Alliance!!!*" Q: "Picard, Picard!! Don't be so daft. This is nothing as inconsequential as you being subjected to interrogation and psychological torture. This is about the fate of your universe...*look!*" Q points up towards a spot in the blue sky. As Picard looks in the direction he is pointing towards, shielding his eyes from the sun, he begins to see an orange ripple in the sky. It starts to get bigger, and the sky darkens as it begins to be consumed. PICARD: "What is it?" Q: "It's the Nexus... It's consuming your entire universe." Picard quickly glances at Q. PICARD (unemotionally): "The most recent readings that I have taken of the Nexus show no noticeable increase in its size." Q: "Picard, you might be able to fool the other ape-like creatures of your world, but you and I both know that its size is increasing exponentially. And it is going to consume your universe even sooner than what that boring, monotone robot of yours says it will." PICARD (spits out): "It's a trick!!! The Nexus is not expanding! It is not going to consume the universe! You are a liar!!!" Q snaps his fingers, and they are back in Picard's Ready Room. "I was hoping that the Picard of this timeline might have a little more sense than the one in the original timeline...but it seems that I was wrong. If you care anything about what will happen to your universe and to everything that you hold most dear, then be on the northern continent of Mirolos in precisely 42.1 hours...*and find Captain Kirk!*"

Q snaps his fingers, and he is gone.

~~~~~~

It is the next day, and Picard and Admiral Katheryn Janeway are having tea and coffee at an outdoor café. They are talking in hushed tones about the Nexus and its increasing expansion. PICARD: "...and Data has no clue as to what is causing it, or how to stop it." Janeway looks at him with concern. Picard looks around suspiciously and then leans in towards Janeway. PICARD: "I haven't told anyone this, but yesterday, when I was taking readings of the Nexus, I had a most unusual encounter in my Ready Room..."

JANEWAY (with interest): "Oh, do tell!" PICARD: "I don't know if it was some sort of trap set up by the Empire to test me, or if I was hallucinating..." He looks around before continuing. "I was taken to the future by this...*funny man*...where I got to see the moment when the Nexus started to consume the entire earth. I was watching it from a café similar to this one, and it felt as real as my sitting here with you. I don't know what to make of it, Kathryn. Whether to believe him, or to get my head examined." JANEWAY: "That sounds like more than just a dream—too unusual and too apropos to be just a coincidence. Maybe it was a message from your deeper subconscious mind, and something that you should take seriously." As they get up and start to leave the café, Janeway smiles at him. JANEWAY: "And it wouldn't hurt to get your head examined in the meantime."

Picard is walking by himself down a deserted alleyway in the middle of the night. A man comes out from behind a dumpster that he walks past and follows him from a moderate distance. Another man comes out from around a corner he passes and follows him along with the other man. A few others appear out of nowhere, joining the group. He walks faster, and then starts to run. They run after him. He turns the corner onto another abandoned alleyway, and quickly sees an open doorway filled with amber light. A young man is standing in its frame, calling out his name and beckoning him to come. YOUNG MAN: "Jean-Luc!" Without thinking, he jumps into the doorway towards the beckoning man.

The scene transforms and now Picard is walking along a trail with the young man in a peaceful and austere forest. PICARD: "Thank you for helping me. How did you know my name?" YOUNG MAN: "I have known you for a long time, Jean-Luc. You used to be like a father to me." PICARD: "Who are you?" YOUNG MAN: "You used to know me by the name of Wesley Crusher." PICARD: "I have never known anyone by that name." WESLEY: "Not in this timeline." Picard stops walking. PICARD: "Is this another trap of some sort? I have already told you, I am not—" WESLEY: "This is not a trick, Jean-Luc. The one who calls himself Q was telling you the truth about the Nexus. It will continue to grow and grow until it consumes all of life in all universes: yours, the mirror universe, the realm that I call home...even the space-time continuum of Q's world is in jeopardy." PICARD: "This is another one of your tricks! Get me out of here! I am not a rebel!!" Picard looks around wildly, as if ready to run away. Wesley looks at Picard with a sorrowful expression upon his face. WESLEY: "I am sorry that you have had such a hard life. Growing up as part of a conquered race of the Terran Empire would make anyone suspicious and distrustful. I tell you, there are other parallel realities where life isn't about fear and suspicion, and struggle and strain. In the timeline where I knew you, there was much more kindheartedness and a sense of family in the people around you—" PICARD: "That is all a pipe dream! I don't know what *timeline* you come from, but in my universe, if you don't protect your own back, you don't survive! Everyone around you is waiting for the opportunity to stick a knife in it, and if you are not prepared to protect yourself and to fight back, you're as good as dead." WESLEY: "That is not the Captain Picard that I knew. He was an honest man, and not afraid to stick up for the underdog. He was a man of courage and moral conviction, and he would not hesitate to risk his life for his crew and the people around him. He was a man that I respected and admired deeply." Wesley turns and looks at him deeply in his eyes. "That was the Captain Picard that I knew." As Wesley continues to look at him, a tear rolls down his cheek.

In the next moment, Picard opens his eyes and is lying in his bed.

Janeway appears on a monitor, half asleep in her nightgown. Picard is sitting at a desk in his study in front of the monitor with an intense look upon his face. PICARD: "I am going to Mirolos…first thing tomorrow morning." JANEWAY: "That's in a Terran militarized zone. Have you gone crazy?" PICARD: "Yes…I believe I have." JANEWAY: "What's happened to you? Why this sudden change in attitude?" PICARD: "It's a long story. Let's just say that I am beginning to feel hope for the first time in a long while." JANEWAY: "Who are you, and what have you done with my friend?" She looks at him for a moment, trying to figure him out. JANEWAY: "Well…I am not going to let you die alone."

Janeway and Picard are in an old mining shuttle, disguised as workers, heading towards the planet Mirolos. JANEWAY: "So you really think this *'Q'*—what's his name?" PICARD: "Just Q." JANEWAY: "—is real and not just in your imagination?" PICARD: "I don't know for sure. But he did mention the planet Mirolos, which I had never heard of before, and yet here it is." A small, distant planet appears through the window. JANEWAY: "And you are supposed to find a dead captain from long ago upon this planet? What possible reason could there be that finding him is the key to saving the universe?" She looks at Picard, while he continues looking out the window and operating the ship without responding. JANEWAY: "So it hasn't crossed your mind that this 'Q' might just be some psycho-hallucinogenic chip implanted into your brain by the Empire to draw you into a trap?" Picard continues to watch the planet through the window as it slowly gets bigger. PICARD: "Well…I think we are about to find out." An enormous military cruiser appears above them through the window. CRUISER (through the com): "Unidentified vessel, you are entering a restricted militarized zone. Turn around and leave at once." Picard briefly glances at Janeway, and then turns towards the console. PICARD (sheepishly): "Oh…my apologies." They continue on their vector towards the north continent of the planet. PICARD: "We are just some scouts for the Iradios Mining Company, looking for potential sources of radium-boracite, and our instruments are picking up very high levels of its radioactive signature on the northern continent of this planet." They continue to approach the planet. CRUISER: "If you do not change your course immediately, we will destroy your ship." PICARD (to Janeway): "Flip that switch over there. If we can trick them into believing we are experiencing a malfunction, maybe they will let us make an emergency landing on the planet." Janeway reaches over and flips the switch, and dark smoke starts to emit out of one of the side thrusters. Miralos looms in front of them, while the cruiser pursues them from behind. PICARD (to the console): "We are experiencing an engine malfunction and are not able to change our course and ask—" The shuttle is fired upon, sustaining heavy damage. JANEWAY: "Now we are experiencing a malfunction—*a major one!*" She looks around a moment and then points out the window. JANEWAY: "If we can just get to that cloud layer, maybe we will have a chance…" The shuttle is hit again as it enters the upper atmosphere of the planet. Both engines are streaming incredible amounts of smoke. PICARD: "We are not going to make it! We are going to have to eject!" JANEWAY: "We won't be able to survive at this altitude!" PICARD: "Incoming photon torpedo!!! We have no choice!" Picard pushes the eject button, but it malfunctions. Janeway tries to open the hatch. It does not budge, and then Picard rushes over to help her. Together, they release the hatch, and then the door blows off and they get sucked out right before the shuttle is destroyed.

The military cruiser, still in space, continues firing at them as they fall through the air. As they flip around and around, hurtling towards the planet's surface without any parachutes, they manage to move towards and to grab a hold of each other. They continue their descent, hugging each other as they approach faster and faster towards the ground, while the military cruiser continues firing lasers all around them from space. Behind it, the Nexus, bigger than ever before, moves towards it. It consumes the ship in a fiery explosion as Picard and Janeway continue hurtling towards the surface. Just before they hit the ground, everything around them lights up as it is enveloped in the Nexus.

Picard and Janeway are standing somewhere, hugging each other, cringing, as if expecting to hit the ground. Slowly, Janeway pulls back and looks around, and Picard does the same. There is a subtle difference in their appearances: less scars and strain upon their faces. JANEWAY: "Where are we?" PICARD (looking around): "I don't know…something here seems familiar." JANEWAY: "It feels so wonderful here. Maybe we both are dead, and there really is such a thing as heaven…" She looks around, eyes wide with wonder.

The scene becomes more focused. They are in an old, Victorian house, and there is a decorated Christmas tree nearby. Picard and Janeway are now both subtly wearing Starfleet uniforms. PICARD: "Oh my God, Kathryn! I know where we are." He looks around. PICARD: "I remember!" He continues looking around in awe. PICARD: "I remember everything…" Suddenly, he breaks down crying. Janeway, her face softer, looking around, holds onto Picard, her face showing the unfolding realization of remembering something as well. JANEWAY (while still holding Picard): "My God, Jean-Luc, I remember too…" PICARD (still holding onto Janeway): "I remember how it was…Starfleet…the honor of serving for a greater cause…my crew…my family—" YOUNG BOY: "Hello, Papa!" Picard pulls back from Janeway and looks at the boy. PICARD: "Thomas—oh my God…my son!" He embraces the little boy while other members of his family surround him. Janeway looks upon the scene with a tender smile upon her face. WOMAN'S VOICE: "Come now, children, give your father some space." As they move back a little, Picard's wife, Elise, appears from the kitchen. ELISE: "How nice to see you, Kathryn. Where are your two lovely boys?" There is an uncertain look upon Janeway's face for a moment, and then a look of remembrance. JANEWAY: "Well…I don't know, Virginia…they might be home next d—" TWINS' VOICES: "Hello, mummy!" Two young boys, twins, come running in. JANEWAY: "Leonardo! Julian! Oh, my God, it feels like I haven't seen you for—" She grabs them both in a single swoop and holds onto them tightly.

MAN'S VOICE: "Hello, Kathryn…" Janeway looks up from the boys she is hugging to see an older man. JANEWAY: "Daddy…?" She looks at him for a moment with a slight tender smile upon her face. She stands up and is about to approach and hug him, when she stops, the smile vanishing off of her face. She just stands there, looking at him. FATHER: "What is the matter, darling? Are you O—" JANEWAY: "You! YOU!!!" She pauses for a moment. FATHER: "What is it—" JANEWAY: "You are not my father! You are a… *vile monster!*" FATHER (tenderly): "What is wrong, Kathy?" JANEWAY: "*Do not call me that!* You are not my father! You are not real!!!" Janeway walks towards a window, away from everyone. JANEWAY (subdued): "None of this is real…" Then, firmly: "*None of this is real.*" She looks at Picard. JANEWAY: "None of this is real. Do you see that, Jean-Luc? None of this is real…" Picard looks at her, and then at his wife, and then at all of the children around him…and then he slowly steps back. Picard sees the Christmas decorations on the tree, and they start to sparkle strangely. PICARD: "None of this *is* real, is it?"

As they look at each other, and then around at everyone in the room, it slowly dissolves, and a vast expanse opens up before them. Barely visible in the dark, they see all around them countless rows upon rows of people lying upon what looks like dark stone slabs, as if in comas. They have slight smiles upon their faces, and wisps of light are constantly leaving through the center of their chests up to some indistinct auroric light, way up high above them. JANEWAY: "Where are we?" PICARD: "I don't know." They look around at all of the comatose people around them. PICARD: "I've been here before…" He looks at one of the people slumbering next to him in fascination. As he looks at him, he slowly starts to get sucked into his world…

It's a beautiful day, and there are people lined up along a road. Picard is standing near a finish line, and he sees the man whose face he saw in a coma running a marathon with several other men running near him. As he nears the finish line, he breaks out into the lead and finishes first. Everyone cheers all around him and beautiful, young women come up and kiss him on the cheek…

PICARD: "*NO!!!*" Picard is suddenly back with Janeway, looking at the man in the coma who just won the marathon. There is a bigger smile upon his face now, and the wisps of light leaving his chest are brighter. JANEWAY: "What happened, Jean-Luc?" PICARD: "I am not sure." *(pause)* "All I know…*is that we have got to find Captain Kirk!*"

Picard and Janeway start aimlessly walking around, looking at the different slumbering people all around them. JANEWAY: "We should split up to increase our chances of finding him." PICARD: "I agree." They start to split up, when Picard stops her. PICARD: "Kathryn—" JANEWAY: "What is it?" PICARD: "I have been here once before, but it is so wonderful and realistic, that I fooled myself into believing it once again. What was it about your fath —I mean—whatever that was that gave it away?" JANEWAY: "It's a long story. Suffice it to say, I have met these beings before."

Picard continues in the same direction as Janeway moves off in a different one. As Picard walks along, he stops and looks at the countless numbers of comatose people that seem to go on into infinity. PICARD (mumbling to himself): "There is no way we are ever going to find him." WOMAN'S VOICE: "You are right…at least, not the way you are looking for him." Picard spins around to see Guinan. PICARD: "Guinan! Is that really you?" GUINAN: "If you remember from the last time, I am not really here. I am just an echo of my former self." PICARD: "What are you doing here?" GUINAN: "I have always been here. For me, the last time we saw each other was just a moment ago—" PICARD: "…because time has no meaning here. Yes…" *(eyes widening)* "I remember that." *(pauses as concern shows on his face)* "What is happening to me, Guinan? All of these new memories from some other life keep flooding in…" *(wincing)* "Am I loosing my mind?" GUINAN (smiling compassionately): "You are in the process of integrating with the memories of your echo from a version of yourself that came here from a different timeline—one in which you teamed up with Captain Kirk and saved millions of lives…" PICARD (full of wonder): "Yes, I remember—I…I remember that life was so…meaningful." PICARD (composing himself): "I am looking for Captain Kirk. Can you show me where to find him?" GUINAN: "There are two answers to that question." She pauses for a moment with a slight smile upon her face. GUINAN: "All you have to do is to focus upon his face." Picard closes his eyes, and then in the next moment, he is looking at the comatose body of the original Captain Kirk from the Prime Universe, lying upon a slab. He is smiling slightly, and as Picard transfixes upon his face, he suddenly gets pulled into his reality…

Picard is outside old Kirk's cabin in the woods, looking around, when he sees Kirk come jogging up from a trail. He sees Picard, and stops short. OLD

KIRK: "Am I dreaming? Jean-Luc, is that you, old friend?" PICARD (smiling): "Yes, it is. It is great to see you." Kirk walks up to him, and they briefly hug. OLD KIRK: "What brings you to my neck of the woods? Wait. Don't tell me. You've come because you need me to help you to save the universe once again." PICARD: "Well, in a manner of speaking—" OLD KIRK: "Well, come on in, and tell me all about it! Antonia is probably cooking some eggs right now. I will tell her to throw a few more on the griddle." Kirk walks inside with his arm around Picard's shoulder.

Antonia is cooking eggs in the kitchen. OLD KIRK: "Antonia, dear, I would like you to meet an old friend of mine: Jean-Luc." Antonia wipes her hand upon her apron and reaches out to Picard, smiling. ANTONIA: "Pleased to meet you." Picard shakes her hand a little uneasily, knowing she is not real. He sits down with Kirk at the table. OLD KIRK: "So what have you been up to these days? Any battles with the Klingons lately?" PICARD (still uneasy): "Um…well, no." *(pause)* "Actually, we have been at peace with the Klingons for over 50 years, now." OLD KIRK: "Ah…well, I see." *(pause)* "What about the Enterprise? I bet she's quite a bit—" PICARD: "Jim, we need to talk. Can we go for a walk?" Kirk pauses for a moment, and then responds: "Yes, of course. Let's go. I'll be back in a little bit, Antonia."

They are now outside, walking along a trail in the woods, next to a lake. OLD KIRK: "Isn't she great—Antonia, I mean. I married her, you know. She has been the best thing for me since—" PICARD: "Jim…it's not real. You know that the Nexus is all one big façade." Kirk stops walking along the trail and stares at him. OLD KIRK: "It's real to me. It *feels* real." PICARD: "But it is not. And I need you to come to help me right a terrible wrong." OLD KIRK: "Right a terrible wrong? How many times do I have to keep doing that? You know, after I helped you defeat Soran, I got pulled back here, to the Nexus. I am *happy* here. I finally got to marry the love of my life, and I am doing everything that I have always wanted to do—things that I have never given myself the time to do in the past. What could be so wrong about that?" PICARD: "It is wonderful, Jim, it really is, but—" OLD KIRK: "There are no buts about it. It *is* wonderful, and the universe can and will survive just fine without me." Picard is taken aback for a moment, remembering he had used almost those exact same words with Q. OLD KIRK: "I have more than earned my retirement…and I am going to enjoy it."

~~~~~

Picard is back standing next to Kirk lying upon the slab, quietly regarding him with a troubled look upon his face. The slight smile upon Kirk's face has disappeared, and the wisps of light are not wafting out from his chest as much as they were before. Guinan looks at Picard with a slight smile and a knowing look. GUINAN: "Didn't go too well, I take it?" Picard silently shakes his head as he continues to look at Kirk. GUINAN: "It is not easy to pull people out of their paradises…especially when they make themselves believe that they are real." PICARD: "I am not sure what to do, Guinan. I came here and found Kirk as Q insisted, but to what end?" GUINAN: "Remember when you asked me to show you where to find Kirk, that I said there were two answers to that question?" Picard looks up at Guinan with interest. GUINAN: "Well, there is another one." Picard looks at her in stunned silence. PICARD: "You mean to tell me that there are two Captain Kirks in here?" She continues to stare at him with her coy smile. GUINAN: "Take my hand."

Picard takes her hand, and everything transforms around him. Suddenly, he is in the grandstands among a large, cheering audience, outside next to a ski slope, where different people are racing towards a finish line on snowboards. We hear the song "Sabotage" by the Beastie Boys playing as young Kirk is doing dangerous, death-defying maneuvers going down crazy steep slopes and avoiding numerous obstacles competing against others in a no-holds-barred, extremely violent race. He gets down to the bottom and barely beats out the second-best competitor across the finish line. The audience goes wild as he is handed the trophy by six gorgeous women. He invites them all to his place, which they enthusiastically accept.

Picard looks at Guinan. PICARD: "I've got my work cut out for me, don't I?" She looks at him knowingly. GUINAN: "I would say so."

Picard, dressed in a nice suit, and Janeway, in a respectable dress, are standing on a sidewalk in a quaint residential neighborhood with modestly nice houses, green lawns and large, broad-leafed trees lining the peaceful roadway. A brand-new, cherry-red Mustang convertible is parked in front of the house they are standing near to. The front door to the house opens, and young Kirk comes walking out onto the porch with his mother and father following him. They hug good-bye. FATHER: "I really had a great time, son. Come back soon." YOUNG KIRK: "Thanks for having me." He walks down the stairs towards his car as Janeway and Picard approach him on the sidewalk. PICARD (smiling congenially): "Excuse me—" "YOUNG KIRK: "Hey there. I'm not Mormon." Kirk turns to them as he is getting in his car. "Thanks for thinking of me, though." PICARD: "We're not Mormons." JANEWAY: "We're here because we need your help." Young Kirk is now in his car and already starting it up. YOUNG KIRK: "The Jehovah's Witnesses chapel is just a few blocks down that way." Kirk points down the road, and then puts the car in reverse and starts to back up. PICARD (angrily): "We are not Mormons, Jehovah's Witnesses, or connected with any other religious organization, dammit! We are here because we need you to help us fix a terrible mistake, Jim." Kirk stops backing up, looks at him for a moment, and then turns off the motor. YOUNG KIRK: "How did you know my name?"

~~~~~~

Picard (in the front) and Janeway (in the back) are riding in Kirk's Mustang. The top is down, and he is driving extremely fast and skidding around corners —his normal way of driving. YOUNG KIRK: "So you mean to tell me that this world here is going to consume the *real* universe somewhere out there—" Kirk does an expansive wave of his arm as he skids around a corner sending a distressed Janeway sliding across the back seat. He hits the accelerator as he continues. YOUNG KIRK: "—and it will be something like 300 years in the future from now—" He swerves around another corner, sending Janeway flying in the other direction. JANEWAY: "Are there any seatbelts back here? I think you're going to kill me." YOUNG KIRK: "—but time is somehow irrelevant here because this place isn't real—" He swerves around another corner. YOUNG KIRK: "Oh—and I almost forgot—you two were subjects of the brutal Terran Empire which ruled both the normal universe and the mirror universe…all because of a wormhole somewhere in the Alpha quadrant?" He swerves around another corner, and then guns it down a straightaway dirt road out in the middle of nowhere. YOUNG KIRK: "Did I get all of that right?" Janeway's face is ghostly white, while a very stiff Picard is sitting upright with a strained expression upon his face. PICARD: "Yes, that's about it." Kirk looks over at Picard as he continues flying down the straightaway, gaining more speed. YOUNG KIRK: "Did Joe put you up to this? He put you up to this, didn't he? I am going to just—" JANEWAY (pointing ahead): "LOOK OUT!!!" Kirk swings his head around and sees a man standing right in the middle of the road. In the next flash, he slams on the breaks and jerks the wheel to the left, off of the dirt road and over brambles and rocks as he skids to a stop, leaving a cloud of dust all around them. YOUNG KIRK: "What the hell?!?" As he looks around, old Kirk walks through the cloud of dust up to his door. YOUNG KIRK: "What the hell do you think you are doing, old man?!? You could have gotten us all killed!!!" JANEWAY (mostly to herself): "Funny, that's exactly what I was thinking." YOUNG KIRK: "And look at what you did to my car! It's all scratched up!" Old Kirk shakes his head as he continues to look at him. OLD KIRK: "I can't believe what an arrogant asshole I was back then." Picard and Janeway give each other a knowing look. Young Kirk stares at him with an exasperated look upon his face: "Who the hell are you?!?" OLD KIRK: "That's right…we haven't been introduced. Pleased to meet you. My name is James Tiberias Kirk."

~~~~~~

Young Kirk, old Kirk, Janeway, Picard, and Guinan are all standing among the slabs of sleeping bodies. YOUNG KIRK: "So you mean to tell me that I am not really dead, then?" GUINAN: "No, you are not. You entered the Nexus while you were still alive. They tricked you into believing that you were dead so that they could keep you trapped here." YOUNG KIRK: "I should have known." *(pause)* "The moment that they said I was in heaven, I should have known that they were lying." Guinan, Picard, Janeway, and old Kirk all look at each other, but don't say anything. YOUNG KIRK: "So because I am still alive, I can go back to whatever time and place I want?" GUINAN: "That's right." YOUNG KIRK: "And if we don't stop the Empress of the Terran Empire and destroy that wormhole, the whole universe will be consumed by this—whatever this thing is?" GUINAN: "Yes, basically." He points to old Kirk. YOUNG KIRK: "And am I really going to look like that when I get as old as him?" OLD KIRK (to himself): "And this is what I left paradise for…" YOUNG KIRK: "So, in a nutshell, it's up to us to save the universe." Old Kirk, Janeway, and Picard look around at each other, and then back to young Kirk. All three answer simultaneously: OLD KIRK: "Yep." JANEWAY: "That's right." PICARD: "You got it." He looks at them all for a moment. YOUNG KIRK: "Then what the hell are we waiting for? Let's kick some Terran ass and go save the universe!" OLD KIRK: "Well…the problem is—" A man's voice interrupts from out of the darkness: "…you don't know how to do it."

A tall, hooded figure walks towards them from out of the darkness. As he approaches, he pulls back his hood, revealing the face of Ambassador Spock. There is a slight hue or glow to him. *(Note: This is a computerized rendition of old Spock, similar to what was done with Princess Leah in* Rogue One.*)* OLD KIRK: "Spock…is that really you?" OLD SPOCK: "If you are wondering as to whether I am part of the façade created by the Nexus, then I can tell you that I most assuredly am not." YOUNG KIRK: "I was told that you died 18 months ago in my time—I mean before I di—I mean 18 months before I left—I mean—I don't know what I mean…but you understand what I mean." Old Spock looks at him for a moment…and then smiles. OLD SPOCK: "As you so eloquently stated, Jim—I died. On New Vulcan on stardate 2263.02, to be exact. In that moment, the Nexus was passing near our solar system, and was close enough to draw my katra—or what you call your soul—to it. I saw old friends and deceased family members waiting for me there, upon a New Vulcan that was a paradise compared to the old one that is gone forever. I, too, was fooled for a period of time by this illusion that seems so real. But I soon became aware of what it really is, and have since moved on. I have come back here to help you prevent the expansion of the Nexus from taking over the entire universe, but I fear that our time will be short, as my presence will have undoubtedly alerted the beings of light that control this realm." OLD KIRK: "Who are these light beings, Spock?" OLD SPOCK: "There is not much time to explain. All I can tell you, is that they are a group of ancient ethereal beings called the Nephilim—" OLD KIRK: "The Nephilim of the Bible?" OLD SPOCK: "That religious text does indeed talk about the historical beginnings of this race, but it does not talk about what has happened to them, or what they have evolved into. These Nephilim are the most dangerous and nefarious beings in the entire universe." JANEWAY: "I remember them. I had a close encounter with death once, and they—*or it* —appeared as my father. It knew everything about me: how I thought, my deepest yearnings…even things I hadn't told anyone. It was so real…" OLD SPOCK: "These entities use deception to lure consciously aware beings like ourselves into their trap to feed upon our emotions. Emotion is one of the few things in the universe that can tap into the unlimited energy of the quantum vacuum and free it up. The amount of energy that emotion can generate is immense, and because of this, the combined energy that the Nexus is generating from everyone that they have lured into it is so incredibly vast, that it can distort the fabric of space, and even time itself. But the energy of emotions is so subtle and ethereal, that it is almost impossible to detect in our universe. Being from another realm, they know how to harness and to use that energy for their own purposes. When they lure someone into their matrix, not only do they feed off of their emotional energy, but they also have access to all of the knowledge and the wisdom that they have accumulated throughout their entire life. These entities are very old, and they have accumulated enough technological information from all of the different species that they have trapped in their matrix to be able to assemble an armada that could conquer the entire universe, should they ever be able to enter it. They have been waiting for countless millennia for a window to open up from our world into theirs. This opportunity appeared to them when the Empress of the Terran Empire, Hoshi Sato, stumbled upon a very specific high frequency of polarized light, that when shot at perpendicular angles to each other, creates a holographic aperture through which she has been able to communicate with them. These beings of light have been sharing small bits of technological information with her in exchange for setting up ultra-dimensional beacons around populated worlds. These beacons are connected to the Nexus, and attract people to them at death, where the Nephilim lie in wait to lure them in. These beings of light can tap into your mind and know exactly who to portray to get you to follow them into their matrix. They can disguise themselves as deceased family members, old friends that have passed away, religious leaders and saints—even God and heaven itself, as a bright light, singing angels, or in whatever form a person imagines it to be." Spock pauses to look at them all, assessing the impact of his words. OLD SPOCK (continuing): "For most people, right after they die, they are in a state of shock, and it makes it very easy for these entities to deceive people at a time when they are the most vulnerable." YOUNG KIRK: "Heck, I wasn't even dead, and yet they still tricked me into believing it was all real." OLD SPOCK: "These entities feed upon other people's emotions by creating a false world around them. Each person that gets trapped in the Nexus feeds it and makes it stronger, increasing its magnetic attraction. Eventually, if the Nexus reaches a critical mass, it will be so powerful that it will suck every living being into it at death, no matter how far away they are, and it will continue to grow like a cancer until it consumes the entire universe. These beacons must be destroyed at all costs, and one of you must convince the Empress of this. The other thing that must be done, is that you must destroy her wormhole leading into your universe. She will never let you do this willingly, as she has every intention of conquering both universes now that she has the technological advantage. One of you will have to do this from her side of the wormhole. You must detonate a polaron torpedo with the precise frequency of 11.323 terahertz in order to destroy it."

Spock turns to young Kirk. OLD SPOCK: "Jim, you must go back to the point in time just before the Empress destroys the Federation fleet and takes control of both universes. When you see my younger counterpart, you must convince him that it is really you. I can tell you, it will be no easy task, as I, especially then, will not believe that someone could come back after being dead for so long. And to him, there is no doubt in his mind that you died that day when the Nexus captured you." YOUNG KIRK: "I will find a way—" OLD SPOCK: "You must, and it is imperative that you tell him to change his shield frequencies to 1.14 gigahertz. That will make you immune to the Empress' weapons." PICARD: "And how do we destroy the Nexus, once and for all?" OLD SPOCK: "Unfortunately, there is no weapon in your universe that is capable of destroying it. The Nexus can only be destroyed when every last sentient being within it sees it for what it really is and departs it of their own, free will."

Lights start flashing way up high, back and forth like faraway lightning. They all look up. OLD SPOCK: "This will be no doubt the last time that anyone alive will be able to enter the Nexus, ever again. They have already started putting measures in place that made it extremely difficult even for me to come back to give you this message." The lightning flashes again. OLD SPOCK: "They are coming. You all must hurry." Spock looks at Old Kirk with a noticeable tenderness in his eyes. OLD KIRK: "I can't go back, can I?" OLD SPOCK: "No, my old friend, you cannot. Your body died when you helped Captain Picard prevent Soran from destroying the Veridian star system and the millions of people inhabiting its fourth planet." They all look at Old Kirk with tenderness. More lightning, closer this time. Young Kirk goes over and shakes old Kirk's hand. YOUNG KIRK: "It's been an honor." After a pause: "I am sorry I acted like such an insolent asshole towards you." OLD KIRK: "Oh, just burning off some old karma, I'm sure." He pats him on the shoulder, smiling. "Forget about it." Ground-shaking lightning. OLD SPOCK: "We must go."

He looks at old Kirk: "My dear friend, are you up for one final mission?" OLD KIRK: "Will it be dangerous?" OLD SPOCK: "Most certainly." OLD KIRK: "Will it be immensely difficult?" OLD SPOCK: "Without a doubt." OLD KIRK: "And will I be up against almost insurmountable odds?" OLD SPOCK: "Absolutely." He pauses a moment. OLD KIRK: "I thought you'd never ask."

[Mirror universe, 22nd century, stardate 2161.4]
Picard (in a Starfleet uniform) is in a torture chamber. Electric jolts are going through his body as he grimaces in pain. Then they stop. The Empress stands before him as he bends over, gasping for breath. EMPRESS: "Tell me the truth, how did you get here?" PICARD (grimacing): "I told you, I am from the 24th century, and—" EMPRESS (sarcastic): "—you just left the Nexus, a

horrible, energy-sucking deathtrap that lures people into it after they die." PICARD: "You must destroy the beacons that you have been placing around your planets. It is what feeds the Nexus—" The Empress quickly nods to an assistant, who pushes a button. Jolts of electricity are heard as Picard writhes in pain. With a nod from the Empress, he releases the button, and then it stops. EMPRESS: "That is classified information!!! How did you find out about them?!? They are not beacons! Our researchers have tested them, and they have found no signals coming off of them!" PICARD (panting and in pain): "They are not directed at the living..." EMPRESS: "You expect me to believe that these *beacons*, as you call them, are pulling dead people into the Nexus?!? What do you take me for??? Our researchers have been monitoring it for almost 50 years now, and they have found no noticeable increase in its size!" PICARD (still panting): "In the future that I came from, it started increasing in size shortly after you placed those devices around all of the inhabited planets...in both of our universes." The Empress smiles. EMPRESS: "In *both* of our universes...? So, if you are right, I am about to become the Empress of two universes—" PICARD (panting): "It is a grave mistake...if you destroy the Federation, you will play right into their plans... it will be the end of us all..." A nearby console with a viewscreen turns on, showing the face of an officer on the Bridge. OFFICER: "Empress, we are detecting scans in the vicinity of the test site from the other side." EMPRESS: "Open up the wormhole. I will be there shortly." OFFICER: "Yes, Empress." The viewscreen turns off as the Empress turns towards the assistant. EMPRESS: "Find out what he knows." As she walks out, electric, buzzing noises start and Picard is heard screaming.

~~~~~~~

[Normal universe, 23rd century]
We see the *Enterprise-A* as it is moving through space. It looks ragged and dilapidated as it moves towards the rendezvous point where the USS *Defiant* awaits. YOUNG SPOCK'S VOICE: "Captain's log, stardate 2269.5. On our way back to Earth, after completing our five-year mission exploring the Robidian Nebula, we have just received orders to rendezvous with the rest of Starfleet to address the new threat of the Terran Empire, which has commandeered one of our own ships, the USS Defiant, and has destroyed another. Despite their weariness from being out in space for so long, my crew has been tried and tested, and I trust that we will be able to eradicate this threat swiftly and effectively..."

~~~~~~~

Young Spock is on the Bridge with the rest of the crew. Young Kirk is there, being held by two security guards, Hendorff and Giles. YOUNG SPOCK: "Place him in the brig." HENDORFF: "Yes, sir!" The two security guards start pulling young Kirk off of the Bridge. He breaks away for a moment and is able to run back in front of Spock. YOUNG KIRK: "Spock, it's me! I'm not dead! You've got to believe—" YOUNG SPOCK: "I do not believe in fairy tales of people coming back from the dead after five years." Kirk is grabbed by the two security guards again and is being pulled towards the door. YOUNG KIRK: "It's a trap! You need to—" YOUNG SPOCK: "I do not know who you are, or how you got onto my ship, but I most certainly will not be taking orders from you—" YOUNG KIRK (being pushed out as the door is closing behind him): "It's a trap! You need to change your shield frequencies to 1.44—"

~~~~~

Kirk is being roughly handled as he is being escorted by the security guards down a corridor to the brig. YOUNG KIRK (to Hendorff): "Why is it always you?" Hendorff continues pushing him down the corridor without responding when young Scott comes from the other direction. YOUNG SCOTT: "Capt'n Kirk?!? *Is that you???*" YOUNG KIRK: "Scotty! We're falling into a trap! We've got to change our shield frequencies to 1.14 gigahertz, or we'll be destroyed!" The security guards continue pushing Kirk past Scott down the corridor. He just stands there with his mouth open. YOUNG SCOTT (to himself): "Was thot really Capt'n Kirk?"

~~~~~

[Mirror universe, 22nd century]
The Empress enters the Bridge of her mother ship. It is darker and larger than any Bridge and with more crew members than ever seen on a Federation ship. The Empress walks over to her chair, which is throne-like and raised up significantly higher than everyone else. In front of her is a podium-like structure with a large symbol of the Terran Empire upon it. OFFICER: "Empress, Captain Zerthos has destroyed the Federation ship, USS Excelsior, and has taken position on the other side of the wormhole in their universe." EMPRESS: "Excellent. When the lambs are ripe for the slaughter, tell him to inform me at once." An officer, Yazin, appears on a console that has risen near her left arm. YAZIN: "Empress, something unusual is happening with the holocommunication device. You are going to want to see this."

~~~~~

[Normal universe, 23rd century]
The *Enterprise* is continuing towards its rendezvous point in Tholian space. Young Spock is on the Bridge, talking with an officer at a console. The doors open and McCoy enters, breathless. He sees Spock and rushes up to him. YOUNG MCCOY: "Scott just told me that he saw Kirk being escorted to the brig. Is it true, Spock? Is he really back?" YOUNG SPOCK: "As you know, Doctor, Mr. Scott is prone to exaggeration, and likely believes in such fictitious characters as Leprechauns." YOUNG MCCOY: "Is it *true*, Spock?" YOUNG SPOCK: "Captain Kirk has been dead for five years, now, Doctor. That man sitting in our brig is an impostor." YOUNG MCCOY: "So he is back! I knew he wasn't dead!" YOUNG SPOCK: "I would expect that you, of all people, Doctor, would not be so gullible as to get sucked into one of Mr. Scott's fantastic fairy tales. There is no logical scenario that could include any possibility of Captain Kirk being alive right now." YOUNG MCCOY: "Damn your Vulcan logic, Spock! There are things in this universe that can't simply be explained away with a little bit of wishful thinking!" YOUNG SPOCK (annoyed): "Wishful thinking? You think that I *wish* Captain Kirk is dead?" YOUNG MCCOY: "I'm just sayin', Spock, we don't really know what the Nexus is. There were reports of people in bliss before they got pulled out of there. Who's to say that there couldn't be a way for a person to survive inside of it?" *(pleading)* "At least let me see him, Spock. If it is him, I will know." YOUNG SPOCK: "We are due to rendezvous with the rest of the fleet and to confront the Terran Empire in less than twelve minutes. There is no time to be chasing ghosts right now, Doctor." YOUNG MCCOY (angrily): "Take a look around, Spock! You have been pushing this crew far longer than any captain in their right mind would have done. If you would come out of that little box of logic that you've been hiding in, you would see that the crew is ready to tear each other apart. Heck! Lieutenant Uhura hasn't even said one word to you in over three months, much less look at you—" YOUNG SPOCK (slowly building anger): "My personal relationships have nothing to do with—" YOUNG MCCOY (emphatically): "Your personal relationships have everything to do with what is happening with this crew! You should have ended our mission into the Robidian Nebula long ago...but everyone knows that you kept going, pushing the crew and the ship out of guilt for having abandoned Captain Kirk when he needed you the most—" YOUNG SPOCK (anger building): "Vulcans are incapable of experiencing guilt—" YOUNG MCCOY: "Dammit Spock!!! You're not just Vulcan. You're human, as well!" *(calmer)* "All that I am saying, Spock, is that if it really is Captain Kirk sitting in that brig right now, this crew needs him more than ever before... At least let me take a blood sample so that we can know

for sure." YOUNG SPOCK (restrained anger): "Perhaps what is really going on, Doctor, has nothing to do with my *relationship* with the crew. Perhaps it is really your own projection onto me of your own self-loathing and hatred..." McCoy's face turns red with anger as he looks at Spock. YOUNG SPOCK: "You are welcome to chase will-o-the-wisps on your own time, Doctor. But right now, you are needed in Sickbay." YOUNG MCCOY (seething): "You green-blooded...inhuman... pointy-eared...*hobgoblin!* I think you really do wish he was dead so that you don't have to face the guilt that you have been hiding from all this time!"

McCoy turns and briskly walks off of the Bridge. Spock, affected by his last statement, masks his inner conflict by resuming his conversation with the officer at the console.

[Mirror universe, 22nd century]
Picard is sitting on the floor of a prison cell, his head in his arms and around his knees. A prison guard opens the door and Picard looks up. GUARD: "The Empress has summoned you. Get up!" As Picard is standing up, wounds show on his body and upon his face. He is grabbed roughly and pulled out.

Picard is shoved into a large room with the holocommunication device in the center of it. Upon entering, the Empress screams at him. EMPRESS: "What have you done to my holowindow???" PICARD: "I have no idea what you are talking about—" EMPRESS (yelling): "He is asking for you—" OLD KIRK'S VOICE: "Jean-Luc, old friend, is that you?" PICARD: "Jim...?" Picard walks over to the device and sees a holographic image of old Kirk. His image is glowing, but there is also color to him, unlike the Nephilim. Far off in the background, thousands of different beings, including humans, Vulcans, Andorians, and Teenaxians, all in color and all faintly glowing, are seen chaotically moving around and randomly disappearing while more appear. EMPRESS: "You sabotaged my device, Picard!!!" OLD KIRK: "Manners, now, Empress. That is not the proper way to be a good host—" EMPRESS: "*Silence!!!*" OLD KIRK (to Picard): "I have been trying to teach her good manners and proper etiquette, but I fear it is all for naught—" EMPRESS (yelling): *"What have you done with the others?!?"* OLD KIRK: "Oh, you mean those nasty, life-sucking vampires that you think are your friends? I haven't done anything with them. Not directly, anyway." A smug little smile appears on old Kirk's face. OLD KIRK: "There is a little bit of a revolution going on in the Nexus right now, Empress, so they might be a bit distracted." PICARD (smiling): "You have gotten them all to see the Nexus for what it really is!" OLD KIRK: "Good heavens, no! For most people here, it is like trying to pull teeth, and believe me when I say, they do bite back. It was an understatement when Spock said this final mission wouldn't be easy. Most people would rather hold onto their illusions of comfort and security than to be free. But…I got a few to listen. And some of them got a few others to wake up. And they, in turn, woke up a few more…" EMPRESS: "This is a trick, Picard! If you don't remove this *virus* at once, I will wipe out every last person in your precious little Starfleet!" OLD KIRK (angrily): "What gives you the right to kill millions of innocent people?" EMPRESS: "I am the empress of the Terran Empire! I don't have to explain my actions to you!!!" OLD KIRK: "So you feel no guilt whatsoever slaughtering millions of lives?" EMPRESS: "Our one true Lord, Terovah, ruler over all creation, has declared that we are a superior race and has given us the mandate to conquer and subdue all living beings and to have dominion over them…" *(becoming zealous)* "We are His chosen people—" OLD KIRK: "At least as long as you continue to worship him—" EMPRESS (angrily): "You don't know anything! It is our God-given right to rule over the entire universe and He has told us to slay anyone who tries to get in the way of what has been promised to us!" OLD KIRK: "It is easy to make promises when one has all of eternity in order to fulfill them…" EMPRESS: "How dare you question the dictates of the Supreme Lord Terovah! You are just some bits of data in a program trying to subvert me from my divine destiny!" OLD KIRK: "Have you ever considered the possibility that your great *God* is just setting you up…? Setting you up to keep you separated from the rest of the world around you…to keep you always struggling to survive and in a constant state of fear…never trusting anyone or anything…never trusting in the inherent goodness of the universe…" EMPRESS: "This is all complete nonsense! Do you think I am a fool, Picard? You are a spy from the Federation, trying to get me to believe in fairy tales and ghost stories in order to subvert me from my true—" A woman's voice is heard from the communication device: "*Hoshi…*"

The Empress stops in mid-sentence, and looks over at the communication device. An exact likeness of her has appeared in the holographic window, but dressed more modestly. OTHER HOSHI: "It is not a ghost story. Everything that they have said is true. I am your counterpart—or was—from the other universe—" EMPRESS (yelling): "You are a fake!" *(after a pause)* "If you really are me—" She starts speaking in the difficult and unusual language of

Yakalaki. EMPRESS: "Tell me, how did you die?" OTHER HOSHI (replying in Zshi'tanga, an even more unusual and crazy-sounding language): "I died in Brazil on 2186, eighty-three years ago in the time frame of the other universe, during a—" EMPRESS (in Xindi-Reptilian): "You lie! This is all a trick to get me to destroy this device—" OTHER HOSHI (in Xindi-Insectiod): "Do you think that Jean-Luc Picard would be able to understand anything that we are saying? We are probably the only two humans in the universe capable of speaking the most difficult dialects of the Xindi…" After a pause, the Empress' face seems to soften a little bit. OTHER HOSHI (in English): "Not everyone in the universe is a liar and a back-stabber. There are good people out there—" EMPRESS: "Good people are weak people, and weak people are dead people!" OLD KIRK: "I feel slighted by that comment." OTHER HOSHI: "You don't always have to have your guard up, Hoshi. Learn to trust. If it wasn't for Captain Kirk here—" OLD KIRK: "Please, call me Jim." OTHER HOSHI (continuing): "—I would still be stuck in that matrix, feeding those monsters. There are good people out there, Hoshi. There are things you can learn from those people in the other universe…" OLD KIRK (to other Hoshi): "They will be coming back soon. We should go." Other Hoshi nods, and starts to fade away. As she does so, OTHER HOSHI: "Trust others, Hoshi. Trust Picard…" Then she disappears.

Then Old Kirk starts to fade away. OLD KIRK (to Picard): "Goodbye, my friend. Eternity awaits…" PICARD: "Wait!" Kirk fades back in for a moment. OLD KIRK: "What is it?" PICARD: "What changed your mind?" OLD KIRK: "When, in the Nexus?" PICARD: "Yes. You had everything you could ever want. What made you decide to want to leave?" OLD KIRK: "I did have everything that I could ever want...and I was happy." After a thoughtful pause: "It truly was heaven there…but I wasn't learning or discovering anything new…I wasn't being challenged…I wasn't growing…*I wasn't making a difference.*" Kirk pauses, thinking for a moment. OLD KIRK: "I was always just taking care of myself, only thinking about my own needs. It started to make my universe feel kind of small. And well…" *(shrugging his shoulders)* "I got bored." After a pause, Kirk starts to fade again. OLD KIRK: "It is time for me to go on a long journey. And I can tell you, that after we die, the adventure does continue… Goodbye, my friend."

As he says this, four original crewmembers, Leonard McCoy *(computer generated)*, Montgomery Scott *(computer generated)*, Nyota Uhura, and Hikaru Sulu appear by his side. Kirk looks over at Sulu. OLD SULU: "Where to, Captain?" OLD KIRK: "Well, I've always wondered what it would be like to visit Risa while being able to see through walls..." OLD UHURA (shaking her head): "Even after death, some things never change." They all turn and start walking towards the swirling blue portal, arms around each other's waists and shoulders. OLD SCOTT: "I think where we're goin' will be way better than any place we can imagine around here, Capt'n." OLD MCCOY: "Where has that pointy-eared bastard run off to, anyway?" They enter the portal and disappear as the holocommunication device turns off.

The Empress looks at Picard for a moment. After a slight pause, she addresses the guard that brought Picard in. EMPRESS: "Leave." The guard leaves, and she is alone with Picard in the room. She turns and walks seductively towards him, lightly touches his head, and then glides her fingers down to his waist. EMPRESS (seductively close): "You know, in my universe, old men who still have it..." She slinks her arms around his waist. "...are the most desirable men of all because they are believed to bring strength and longevity to the family line." PICARD (not resisting): "Well it's too bad I'm not an old man, then." She continues moving her hands across his body seductively. EMPRESS: "That's right! You are a man of the future...more than 150 years my junior!" She continues being seductive, walking behind him while gliding her fingers around his body. EMPRESS: "How did you do it?" PICARD: "How did I do what?" EMPRESS: "Manipulate my holowindow. Did you have someone on the inside help you? Who was it?" PICARD: "Everything I told you was the truth. Those beings you see in that device are not to be trusted, and you must destroy those beacons to protect both of our universes." She slaps Picard across the face. EMPRESS: "You're a liar!!!" Then she softens and seductively moves her hands around his waist as she walks around him again. EMPRESS: "You know, we could be good for each other. You could tell me about things from your time, and I could give you everything you've always dreamed of." Picard does not say anything as she continues walking around him seductively, her hands gliding across different parts of his body. As the Empress moves in front of him, her back facing him, Picard suddenly grabs the phaser out of her holster. Instantly, she whips around and kicks it out of his hand and onto the floor. She dives after it, rolling on the floor. The moment she grabs it, Picard jumps on top of her, pinning her to the floor and knocking the phaser free from her hand. He is still on top of her, with her hands pinned to the floor above her head and her curvaceous body seductively splayed out underneath him. EMPRESS (seductively): "Well, you finally have got me where you want me...now what are you going to do, Captain?" After looking at her for a moment, PICARD: "Your holocommunication device is just too dangerous...I'm sorry, Hoshi." Immediately, Picard jumps off of her, grabs the phaser, and shoots the communication device. Nothing happens. He tries again. Still nothing.

The Empress gets up, nonchalantly walking over and taking the phaser out of his hand. EMPRESS: "My phase pistol can sense who is holding it, and it will only fire when *I* pull the trigger." She points it at him. EMPRESS: "I should kill you for this!" Picard tenses. Then she lowers her pistol and puts it back in her holster. She walks up to him and puts her hands upon his body again. EMPRESS: "But I like men who are feisty like you. Maybe I will put you in my concubine instead...and keep you all for myself!" Picard looks slightly taken aback by this.

A screen from a nearby console lights up with an officer from the Bridge upon it. OFFICER: "Empress. The Federation fleet has arrived." EMPRESS (her hands still on Picard): "Guard!" The prison guard enters the room. She removes her hands and turns to the guard. EMPRESS: "Take the prisoner back to his cell." Then she puts her hands back on Picard for a moment. EMPRESS: "We will have more to discuss later...after I become the Empress of *two* universes!"

~~~~~~

[Normal universe, 23rd century]
The *Enterprise*, along with the rest of Starfleet, is facing the USS *Defiant* sitting in front of the wormhole. Spock is in his chair, looking at Captain Zerthos on the viewscreen. ZERTHOS: "...If you and your fleet surrender at once, we will show you mercy—at least as much mercy as a weak subspecies such as yourselves deserve—" YOUNG SPOCK (emphatic): "We will never surrender." *(turning to Sulu)* "Fire upon that ship with everything we've got!"

Young Kirk is in the brig, pacing back and forth. Hendorff is sitting nonchalantly outside the cell. YOUNG KIRK: "This isn't right. I've got to get out of here!" Suddenly, he almost gets knocked off of his feet as a blast hits the ship. YOUNG KIRK: "*No!!!*" He turns to Hendorff. YOUNG KIRK: "The ship is going to be destroyed! You've got to let me out so I can tell Spock to change the shield frequencies to 1.44 gigahertz!" Another blast hits the ship. Hendorff is still sitting, seemingly oblivious to what is happening all around him. HENDORFF: "Sorry...*Cupcake*. No can do." Kirk turns away and starts beating upon the wall in vain. YOUNG KIRK: "This is all wrong. I've got to get out of here!" As he continues to bang on the wall, he disappears in a transporter beam.

~~~~~

Kirk reappears on the Bridge, looking like he is banging on nothing. He stops in mid-swing, and looks around. The ship is continuing to sustain heavy damage. Crew members are busy working on their consoles as Spock gives orders. Then Spock sees him. YOUNG SPOCK: "What is this person doing on my Bridge?" YOUNG SCOTT (over the com): "I'm sorry, Capt'n! If it really is Kirk, I couldn't just let him sit in thot brig!" YOUNG SPOCK: "I will deal with you later, Mr. Scott. Guards, get this—" Kirk has run up to him by this time, and is speaking directly in his face. YOUNG KIRK: "Spock, you've got to believe me! This is your only chance! You need to change your shield frequencies to—" The guards grab him and start pulling him away. Another blast hits the ship, which causes everyone to stumble, allowing him to get away. Spock is giving different orders to people when Kirk gets back in his face. YOUNG KIRK: "Spock, you need to change the shield frequencies…now!" Spock moves away. YOUNG SPOCK: "Somebody get this man off of my ship!" Spock continues giving out other orders as the ship continues to get rocked with laser fire. Kirk moves up to him and slaps him across the face. YOUNG KIRK: "Spock, you've got to listen to me!" Spock stares at him, and then he loses it, jumping at his throat and pinning him against a console. YOUNG KIRK (barely audible): "Spock, it's me! It's me…" Kirk is about to lose consciousness. YOUNG UHURA (speaking to Spock for the first time in months): "Spock! Stop it!" Startled, Spock slowly removes his hands from Kirk's neck and steps back with a disturbed look upon his face. Kirk starts to cough. SPOCK: "This is disturbingly familiar…" He looks at Uhura, and then around at all of the Bridge crew staring at him. YOUNG SPOCK (talking to no one in particular): "Only one human has ever been able to rile me up into such an irrational state of mind…" He turns abruptly and stares at Kirk in wonder, his face betraying an inner conflict between the logic and intuition battling within his mind. YOUNG SPOCK: "Jim...is it really you?" YOUNG KIRK (barely able to speak): "It's me, Spock." *(after catching his breath)* "You've got to change the shield frequencies to 1.44 gigahertz." Spock continues to stare at him, dumbfounded. A severe blast hits the ship, making everyone stumble. YOUNG KIRK: "*Now!*" Spock snaps out of it. YOUNG SPOCK (to Sulu): "Do as he says." Sulu makes the adjustment, right as another laser blast hits the ship. Everything remains calm. SULU: "The blast had no effect. Shields are holding." YOUNG SPOCK (still staring at Kirk): "Hail the rest of the fleet and let them know the frequency." Uhura does so, and shortly after the ships on the viewscreen show the laser fire having no effect upon them.

YOUNG KIRK (sitting in the captain's chair): "Now hit them with everything we've got, Sulu!"

~~~~~~

A massive battle continues to ensue between the two fleets. The Federation ships show heavy damage, but now the laser fire is not affecting them. The Terran fleet has suffered no damage. Out of the wormhole appears the Empress' ship, larger and more-advanced looking than any other ship there, joining the Terran fleet. The Empress is on her throne, as the crew on her Bridge work their consoles. The huge viewscreen shows her ship moving in next to the rest of the ships in her fleet, firing upon the heavily damaged Federation ships and having no effect. Her ship gets hit by a laser blast. OFFICER: "No damage, Empress. Shields holding at 98%." EMPRESS: "Why are our weapons not working?!? They should have already destroyed the fleet by now! Hail Commander Thanatos!" A viewscreen slides up near her left arm, and Commander Thanatos is seen bowing on it. THANATOS (head slightly bowed): "Empress." EMPRESS: "What is happening??? Why are our weapons causing no damage?!?" THANATOS: "They were working, Empress, and then about three minutes ago, they started having no effect." A blast hits the Empress' ship. OFFICER: "Shields holding at 97%." EMPRESS: "They just stopped working?!? Did it ever occur to you that maybe they know our weapon frequencies?!?" THANATOS: "I did not—" EMPRESS: "*Change the frequencies!!!* Put them on a random rotating frequency and alert the rest of the fleet!"

~~~~~~

Young Kirk is still sitting in the captain's chair on the Bridge of the *Enterprise*. YOUNG SULU: "Captain, our weapons are having almost no effect upon their shields." A laser blast hits their ship, causing no damage. YOUNG KIRK: "I'll take whatever we can, Sulu. If it takes a week of firing upon them in order to drain their shields, then so be it." Another laser blast approaches them, and blows right through their ship, causing heavy damage. Then another. YOUNG KIRK: "Evasive actions, Sulu!" On the viewscreen, other Starfleet ships are seen taking heavy damage, as well. YOUNG KIRK: "Alert the whole fleet to take evasive actions! Keep firing, Sulu!" The *Enterprise* takes another hit. Then the viewscreen shows some of the Starfleet ships being destroyed. A photon torpedo is launched from the Empress' ship, moving straight for the *Enterprise*. YOUNG KIRK: "Evasive actions!!!" The photon torpedo hits, causing explosions, hull damage, and fires. YOUNG KIRK: "Report!" YOUNG SULU: "Shields are down! Breaches on Decks 5 through 24! Weapons and main power are down. One more hit, and we'll be destroyed!" YOUNG UHURA: "A report just in from the rest of the fleet: 11 ships destroyed, 23 have sustained heavy damage—" YOUNG KIRK: "Sulu, put out a fleet-wide transmission to surrender." Everyone on the Bridge stops what they are doing, and looks at Kirk. YOUNG SPOCK: "What, Captain? We can't surr—" YOUNG KIRK: "You were right, Spock. There are times when a captain will have to face a no-win situation. You created the Kobayashi Maru test to show that, and I thought I could cheat it. I was wrong." He turns to Uhura: "Send a transmission to the lead ship that we surrender, and that we will acquiesce to all of its demands."

OFFICER: "Empress, Captain Kirk of the flagship USS Enterprise is signaling its surrender on behalf of all of the Starfleet ships." EMPRESS: "Captain *who*???" Officer: "Captain Kirk. He is the captain of the flagship—" EMPRESS: "Never mind. I will deal with him later. Alert our fleet to immediately cease firing." OFFICER: "Yes, Empress."

Kirk, and the rest of the crew on the Bridge, are watching the viewscreen as the Empress is giving a speech. EMPRESS: "Today will be a day remembered in all of history as the day when our two universes unite—" YOUNG MCCOY: "Unite, my ass." EMPRESS: "—a day when the Terran Empire and the Federation merge together into one, United Empire that will signal the beginning of the greatest civilization that history has ever known…"

The scene switches onto the Bridge of the Empress's ship. EMPRESS: "…and I, Hoshi Sato, shall be the—" OFFICER (cautiously): "Empress—" EMPRESS (extremely annoyed, turning to the officer): "What possible reason could you have to interrupt me in the middle of the most historic speech of—"

The scene switches back to the crew of the *Enterprise* as they watch the Empress on the viewscreen turn to an officer and start talking with him, but they can't hear what is being said. The crew starts talking with each other, wondering what is happening.

The scene switches back to The Empress's ship. OFFICER: "Please forgive me, Empress, but there is a ship signaling us from the other side of the wormhole...in *our* universe." EMPRESS: "In our universe??? What—? *On screen!!!*" Janeway appears on the viewscreen, dressed in ordinary civilian clothes. EMPRESS: "How dare you enter my airspace! Identify yourself immediately!"

The scene switches back to the crew of the *Enterprise* watching the viewscreen as the transmission from the Empress cuts out. YOUNG UHURA: "Captain! I am picking up a transmission coming from the other side of the wormhole." YOUNG KIRK: "Patch it through, Uhura." The viewscreen displays the same transmission that the Empress is receiving coming from Janeway. JANEWAY: "This is Kathryn Janeway of the United Federation of Planets. I have just released a polaron torpedo on the edge of your wormhole in Terran space that will detonate in 60 seconds, closing your wormhole forever. If you and your fleet want to see your precious universe ever again, you had better get back here now!" YOUNG KIRK: "It's Captain Janeway! She's come through!!!" Crew members start cheering on the Bridge.

The scene switches back to The Empress's ship. EMPRESS: "What?? You are delusional! The Tholians have developed this into a stable, bidirectional wormhole, immune to any potential outside acts of sabotage." JANEWAY: "That is quite a feat, in any time frame. Nonetheless, the torpedo I released will detonate at the precise frequency of 11.323 terahertz, disrupting the closed-loop tachyon chains within it resulting in a cascading chain reaction of destabilization. It can—and will—collapse. *You now have 37 seconds.*" EMPRESS (her face red, to an officer): "Order the fleet back into the wormhole. *Now!!!*"

The scene switches to the crew of the *Enterprise* as they watch the Terran fleet on the viewscreen turn around and start heading back through the wormhole, amid more cheering. YOUNG KIRK: "Hail Janeway!" She comes on the viewscreen, smiling. JANEWAY: "Sorry I am late to the party! I hit a few bumps on the road trying to get here." YOUNG KIRK: "Janeway, you did it!" JANEWAY: "No, *we* did it!"

At the same moment, as the last of the Terran fleet passes through the wormhole, it collapses in a brilliant flash of light. As the transmission cuts out, everyone on the Bridge continues cheering.

[Mirror universe, 22nd century]
The Terran fleet has just passed through the wormhole back into their universe. The imposing ship of the Empress is in the middle of them all. A small device is blinking near the edge of the wormhole. EMPRESS: "Destroy that torpedo!!!" OFFICER: "If we hit it with anything, Empress, it will detonate on impact." EMPRESS: "Then beam it away from the wormhole! *Now!!!*" The officer hurriedly works his console. OFFICER: "There is a jamming signal coming off of it that is preventing me from locking onto it." The torpedo detonates and the wormhole starts flashing erratically, about to collapse. The Empress screams at the top of her lungs. As the wormhole flashes erratically on the main viewscreen, it shows Janeway's shuttle far off in the distance. EMPRESS (pointing to the viewscreen): "Destroy that shuttle!"

The fleet starts racing towards Janeway's shuttle. Her eyes widen as she sees them coming. JANEWAY: "Ohhhh...*shit!!!*" She whips the shuttle around and flies away from the fleet as fast as it can go. They chase after her, firing, while the wormhole in the background continues to flash erratically. As Janeway furiously works her console, the flashing wormhole is seen reflecting off of the shuttle's window. JANEWAY: "If I can only get through that wormhole before it collapses." Janeway's shuttle does a sharp about face, and starts weaving through all of the ships, evading being hit. At one point, a laser blast hits the shuttle's right wing, causing it to fly erratically for a moment before it restabilizes. The wormhole does one final flash as the shuttle whips around underneath the Empress' ship, temporarily preventing the Terran ships from firing at her. JANEWAY: "Well, this is it! It's been a wild ride. If I don't make it...I won't regret one minute of it."

The Empress is sitting upon her throne. On the large main viewscreen, the wormhole does one final flash...but then remains. EMPRESS (yelling): "Why hasn't anyone shot down that shuttle yet?!?" At that moment, the shuttle whips up in front of her on the viewscreen, heading directly for the wormhole. EMPRESS: "*Fire upon that shuttle!!!*" Just before the shuttle reaches the wormhole, a laser blast coming from the Empress' ship makes a direct hit. On the Empress' viewscreen, the shuttle is seen exploding right in front of it. As the explosion fades away, and meandering bits and pieces of the shuttle spread out, the viewscreen shows that the wormhole has stopped flashing and now remains stable.

EMPRESS: "Ha! I knew it! The Tholians developed the ability to create a stabilized wormhole that couldn't be destroyed by a simple polaron torpedo. She tricked us!" OFFICER: "Empress, we are being hailed." EMPRESS: "Onscreen!" Seven of Nine appears on the viewscreen. "This is Captain Annika Hansen of the USS Defiant—" EMPRESS (interrupting): "*We* have the USS Defiant!" OFFICER: "Empress, our scans of the wormhole are revealing tachyons with time signatures connected to the—" SEVEN OF NINE: "This is Captain Annika Hansen of the USS Defiant NCC-78633...of the *24th century*. We have detected a Starfleet officer upon your ship. You will release him to us at once." EMPRESS: "This is your Empress, Hoshi Sato. I will not fall for another one of your Federation tricks. You and your crew are now subjects of the United Terran Empire, and you shall surrender your vessel to us at once." SEVEN OF NINE: "The United Terran Empire lasted for a total of 23.4 minutes back in 2269. It is now 2395, and you, Hoshi Sato, no longer rule our universe. If you do not release Captain Jean-Luc Picard of the United Federation of Planets at once, we will fire upon your ship. Your fleet is battle-weary. I have alerted Starfleet of our situation, and more ships will be appearing momentarily. We have had 126 years to prepare for our next encounter, and you are now no match for our weapons. You *will* hand him over... *Resistance is futile*."

An officer leans over, and the Empress signals for the sound to be cut off. OFFICER: "Empress, she is telling the truth. The wormhole now connects us into the other universe 234 years into our future. I have scanned their ship. Their weapons are far superior to the Starfleet ships of the 23rd century. The results would be very uncertain if we were to engage them in a battle right now, and three more ships have already arrived on their side." The Empress's face turns red, and then she screams. She sits back in her chair and breathes deeply while taking it all in. After calming down for a minute, she signals to the officer to turn on the sound. EMPRESS: "I will agree to hand over Jean-Luc Picard, but I deman—I request fifteen minutes before I lower my shields to allow you to transport him back." SEVEN OF NINE: "If he is hurt in anyway—" EMPRESS (resigned): "I just want to say goodbye." Seven of Nine raises an eyebrow. SEVEN OF NINE: "I accept your proposal." As the Empress walks off of the Bridge, she tells an officer to lower the shields in fifteen minutes.

~~~~~

The Empress is in her lavish bedroom. A door opens and a guard escorts Picard into her room, more gently this time, and then leaves. PICARD:

"What is going on? Why am I here?" EMPRESS: "You appear to still have friends in the 24th century, Jean-Luc." PICARD: "*24th century?* What are you talking about?" EMPRESS: "One of your cohorts, a Kathryn Janeway, tried to destroy my wormhole." PICARD (enthusiastically): "Did she succeed?" EMPRESS: "Instead of destroying it, she only managed to shift it into your century." *(angrily)* "But she managed to spoil all of my plans...and she paid for it with her life." PICARD: "What? She's dead?"

Visibly struck, he slowly walks towards the other side of the room. The Empress walks towards him and starts seductively moving a hand across his back. EMPRESS: "She was someone you cared for... You must have been on *very* intimate terms with her." He brushes off her advance and walks away from her. PICARD: "You know...I had a whole lifetime where I lived under the oppression of the Terran Empire. It was drilled into me since I was babe that I was just a human—inferior to the Terrans who ruled over me..." He turns and faces her with a sorrowful expression upon his face. "When you hear it time and time again...all of your life...you really start to believe it..." *(forcefully)* "But I wouldn't let it keep me down. I learned quickly that in order to succeed, you had to step on top of everyone above you—human and Terran alike—until you reached the top...and I did." He continues, almost crying. "I was just like you...I clamored and struggled and connived, until I became the flagship captain of my fleet...but I lost something along the way—"

Picard stops in mid-sentence and walks away. The Empress, visibly affected, slowly walks up to him and cautiously puts a hand upon his shoulder. EMPRESS: "I am sorry." She pauses for a moment. "I had an officer get a report on the current status of the Nexus in my universe. It has shrunk 39% in size in the last 24 hours because of the revolution that Captain Kirk started." Picard turns around to face her. EMPRESS: "It appears that I was wrong about you and your friends and that you were doing something to help save us, after all. I have ordered all of the beacons that I had built to be destroyed." The Empress puts her hands upon his shoulders. EMPRESS: "I am sorry if I caused you any pain...I really thought you were a spy." The Empress looks at him in the eyes for a moment. EMPRESS: "I hope you find what you lost when you get back home..." She reaches up to kiss him on the lips right as he is transported off of her ship.

[Normal universe, 23rd century]
The Bridge of the *Enterprise* is in shambles. Beams and other metal objects lie strewn about upon the floor, wires stick out in random places, and a light smokiness in the air makes the flickering lights even dimmer. Various crew members are milling about looking at the mess around them, while others are working at some of the damaged consoles to see what can be partially repaired. Young Kirk is walking around, looking at the mess around him. Spock and McCoy are nearby, looking around, as well. YOUNG KIRK: "It seems like there is always a mess to clean up around here…" He looks at Spock and McCoy. "Spock, McCoy…walk with me."

[Normal universe, 24th century, stardate 2395.1]
Eight Federation ships are facing the looming wormhole leading into the mirror universe. They are more futuristic looking than anything seen previously in Star Trek episodes or movies. Picard materializes in the transporter room of Seven of Nine's ship. SEVEN OF NINE: "Captain Jean-Luc Picard, it is an honor to finally get to meet you." She steps forward to shake his hand. He doesn't respond. There is a distant look in his face, as if he is not really there. She stops mid-motion. SEVEN OF NINE: "Is everything OK, Captain?" The distant look on Picard's face evaporates. PICARD: "My apologies." He steps forward and shakes her hand smiling. PICARD: "It is a pleasure to meet you. I have heard so many wonderful things about you from—" A dark look appears on his face. SEVEN OF NINE: "Captain?" PICARD: "I'm sorry. I've lost a dear friend today." JANEWAY'S VOICE: "And who might that be?" Picard turns to see Janeway appearing from a corridor. PICARD: "Kathryn?" He rushes over and hugs her. PICARD (after looking at her for a moment): "Hoshi—the Empress—told me you died." JANEWAY: "I surely would have if it were not for stellar actions of my former science officer." SEVEN OF NINE: "I was simply doing what any able-bodied Starfleet captain would have done—" JANEWAY: "…what any Starfleet captain with Borg reflexes would have done."

[Normal universe, 23rd century]
Young Kirk, Spock, and McCoy are walking down a corridor. It looks just as disheveled as it did on the Bridge, with beams, wires, and other parts of the ship lying around in random places. YOUNG KIRK: "So, how did you like being captain of the Enterprise for five years, Spock?" Spock pauses for a moment before answering. YOUNG SPOCK: "Let's just say that I have a greater respect for it. After having the experience…I am quite happy to give it

back to you, Captain." Young Kirk and McCoy exchange a smile as they continue to walk down the corridor, occasionally stepping over various objects strewn about. YOUNG MCCOY: "What was the Nexus like, Jim? Is it as blissful as they claim it to be?" Kirk smiles and shakes his head a little. YOUNG KIRK: "It was like being on the greatest high that you could ever imagine...except there were no hangovers to deal with. It felt so wonderful there, that you made yourself believe it was real, even if things were staring at you right in the face that clearly were not." YOUNG MCCOY: "What do you mean, Jim?" YOUNG KIRK: "Well, it was sort of like being in a dream, where you don't question anything...like my mom, for example." YOUNG MCCOY: "What about your mom?" YOUNG KIRK: "Well, she was there, greeting me at the pearly gates, so to speak...but she isn't dead. Everything felt so incredible and real there, that I didn't even question why she was there."

[Normal universe, 24th century]
Picard, Janeway, and Seven of Nine are walking down a corridor. Janeway and Picard have their arms around each other. JANEWAY: "It was really a stroke of luck that the USS Defiant was making scans of this area when the wormhole from the mirror universe opened into this time frame. I think Annika had literally about 1/10,000th of a second after the wormhole appeared to detect my biosignature and to beam me out before my shuttle blew up. How was it that you just happened to be in the area when that wormhole appeared?" SEVEN OF NINE: "Let's just call it a hunch." Janeway stops and looks at her for a moment. JANEWAY: "A hunch? Knowing you, Seven, something tells me it was more than just a hunch." They continue walking. SEVEN OF NINE: "I have been fascinated with the history of this battle since it happened 126 years ago, and have been studying this region of space for quite a long time now, especially since you and Captain Picard mysteriously disappeared 13 years ago." JANEWAY: "Has it been that long? Well, at least it is good to know that the Empire is no match for our ships in this century." SEVEN OF NINE: "I would not say that, Admiral. We are more evenly matched than I might have led on." Janeway stops and looks at her again before continuing walking. SEVEN OF NINE: "We have more sophisticated scanning technology than we did 126 years ago, and it is clear that their weapons, and especially their shields, are more powerful than we previously had thought. Should we ever have to engage them in a battle, there would likely be heavy casualties on both sides." Janeway looks at Seven of Nine and then shakes her head, smiling. JANEWAY: "I will be sure never to play poker with you, Seven." SEVEN

OF NINE: "I fail to see the relevance of a game of cards to this conversation." Picard and Janeway exchange a smile with each other. PICARD: "Kathryn, how did you manage to procure a shuttle along with a polaron torpedo in their universe?" JANEWAY: "Well, that's a long story. Remember, though, I had a whole lifetime of being a subject of the" *(humorous tone)* "United Terran Empire, and during that alternate lifetime, I lived on the Terran Earth in the mirror universe for three years. Anyway, I got there six months before the battle and—" Picard stops as they pass by an open room with the Empress' holocommunication device in it. PICARD: "What? How did this get here?" A smug smile appears upon Seven of Nine's face. SEVEN OF NINE: "Admiral Janeway informed me of the importance of this device, and so when they lowered their shields in order to beam you out...I decided that the Empress no longer needed it."

[Normal universe, 23rd century]
Young Kirk, Spock, and McCoy enter the Engineering Section of the ship. Everything is in complete shambles there. Scotty is standing there, looking at the mess around him. YOUNG KIRK: "Scotty! When can we get this ship ready for our next mission?" YOUNG SCOTT (humorous): "There is something still not quite right with the warp nacelles. She's a wee-bit fussy of a lass. It could take two weeks to get her purrin' properly again." YOUNG KIRK: "We don't have two weeks, Scotty. We need to get started on our new mission as soon as possible." YOUNG SCOTT: "Well, at least give me another week, Captain... It would be a shame to get out into deep space, only to find that the cylinders aren't all firin' properly." YOUNG SPOCK: "Captain, it will take at least four months to completely fix this ship, if it is even repairable at all." Kirk winks at Scott. YOUNG KIRK: "Nonsense, Spock! I have my full confidence that Mr. Scott here will have our ship up and running at peak performance in one week." Spock looks perplexed as McCoy leans up to his ear. YOUNG MCCOY: "It's a joke, Spock. Play along with it." YOUNG KIRK: "So, where shall we go, Spock, once we have everything up and running again?" YOUNG SPOCK: "Anywhere you like, Captain. Anywhere, that is...except for the Robidian Nebula."

[Normal universe, 24th century]
Picard, Janeway, and Seven of Nine are in the room with the holo-communication device. SEVEN OF NINE: "Even the Borg were not familiar with this technology. How does it work?" PICARD: "I think it uses some very specific, extremely-high frequency of polarized light. It has to be tuned to exactly—" The device starts to light up, as if it is turning on. PICARD:

"What?? There is no energy source here to power it. That's not possible—" SEVEN OF NINE (to her combadge): "Emergency beam out of the device in Cargo Bay One!" As she says this, the window lights up, and Ambassador Spock appears, somewhat faint and distorted. OLD SPOCK: "Jean-Luc..." PICARD: "Spock, is that really you?" SEVEN OF NINE (to her combadge): "Belay that order. Await further instructions." The image of Spock gets sharper. OLD SPOCK: "Yes, it is I. I cannot communicate with you for long, as it takes an enormous amount of energy for me to power this device." PICARD: "We did it, Spock! The universe has been restored to the way it was. And thanks to Captain Kirk and the revolution that he started, the Nexus is even smaller than it was before." OLD SPOCK: "It is true that the Nexus has diminished in size considerably after Captain Kirk helped countless numbers of beings to realize its true nature...but do not think that it is not a threat anymore. It has since stabilized, and has even increased in size somewhat since then. As long as this communication device is still around, there is always the chance that it could get into the wrong hands, and the Nephilim could use it to forward their agenda, once again. I cannot stress enough, that this device needs to be destroyed immediately." PICARD: "I will see to it myself." *(after a pause)* "Did you know?" OLD SPOCK: "Did I know that by detonating the polaron torpedo at the exact frequency that I gave you would shift the wormhole to this time frame?" PICARD: "Yes." Spock smiles slightly. OLD SPOCK: "To within certain tolerances." PICARD: "Why here? Why not destroy it completely?" Spock pauses for a moment, as if thinking about how best to answer. OLD SPOCK: "In looking back at all of the challenging and not-so-pleasant experiences that I have had in my life as a Vulcan, there is one thing that has become clear to me. And that is that life isn't about safety and security. It is about risk and opposition, and through that opposition, one gets opportunities to grow that would otherwise never occur. Our darker halves are not necessarily something to be avoided. To use an old aphorism: 'One cannot live without the other.' You both have enormous powers—the power of wondrous creation...and the power of terrible destruction. There are hidden aspects within each of you, treasures that you both have, waiting to be discovered within each other. The human race has gone far as a species, but there is so much more that it has yet to attain. Your potential is far greater than even I can conceive of...and the key lies with your counterparts in the Dark Universe."

Spock makes momentary eye contact with each person in the room. OLD SPOCK: "It is time for me to go. Now that I have a very different understanding about life and death, instead of saying my customary salutary farewell, I will just say—" Spock raises his hand in the common Vulcan sign. "Live long…and live *on*." Spock slowly disappears, and then the machine shuts down.

The End.

If you are from Paramount Global and you wish to turn my script into a movie, you can contact me at: precisionpyramids@gmail.com. If you are from Paramount Global, and you wish to sue me instead, you can contact me at: this-is-my-real-email-address-it-really-really-is-truly-i-am-not-lying@gmail.com.

Printed in Great Britain
by Amazon